CW01021617

The End of Purgatory

Brandy M. Miller

40 DAY WRITER LLC
DALLAS, TEXAS
HTTP://WRITEYOURBOOK.TODAY

©2020 Brandy M. Miller. Published by 40 Day Writer LLC.

All rights reserved. No part of this publication may be reproduced, distributed, or transmitted in any form or by any means, including photocopying, recording, or other electronic or mechanical methods without the prior written permission of the publisher, except in the case of brief quotations embodied in critical reviews and certain other non-commercial uses permitted by copyright law.

For permission requests, email with a subject line of "Attention: Permissions Coordinator" at the address below:

40daywriter@gmail.com

eBook ISBN: 978-1-948672-20-7

Paperback ISBN: 978-1-948672-21-4

Any references to historical events, real people, or real places are used fictitiously. Names, characters, and places are products of the author's imagination.

Front cover image by Brandy M. Miller

Interior design by Brandy M. Miller

Printed in the United States of America

First printing: 2020.

40 Day Writer LLC

Dallas, Texas

http://writeyourbook.today

Dedication

Dedicated to my sister, Tiffany, and to my nieces: Tosha, Kristina, Amber, Brocke, Ali, Bre, Jocelyn, and Charlotte, as well as to the women who encouraged me to publish this: Glenda, Kathy, and Becky.

Table of Contents

Chapter 1

Zhara shrugged and stared out the window, refusing to meet his eyes. She was about to lie to him, and she didn't want to see his face when she did.

"I like men who know how to handle themselves in a fight. I like men who aren't afraid to break the rules if the occasion calls for it. I like men who like to take risks. I suppose I do have a type. I suppose I do like the bad boy. The one who is the hardest to love, the one who is most likely to leave me."

John came up behind her and stood close enough that she could feel the waves of heat radiating from his body. She knew that if she wanted it all she had to do was rock backward a half an inch and she could be wrapped in his arms. She felt his breath on the back of her neck and closed her eyes. The temptation was there. It would be so easy to give into it.

His question was soft but his words hit her heart hard. "And what about me? Am I your type?"

She forced a laugh. Better to hurt him a little now than to watch him bleed for her later. "You? No. You're much too safe. Much too ordinary. Much too easy to tame. I don't think you could handle me.

I'd crush your spirit and leave you broken."

It was a partial truth. She didn't think he could handle her. Not the real her. She would never let him close enough to find out. He mattered too much. "Oh, really? Am I? Do you think I'm easy to tame? Do you think you know me so well?"

She did know him. Maybe better than he knew himself. She knew he was kind and gentle and generous in a world that had no room for such things. She hardened herself, saying the words that she knew would go straight to that giant heart of his and pierce it straight through. It was the only way to protect him from her.

"I know you better than you think I do. You love me already and I haven't given you any reason to love me. I didn't have to. You love everything about me, but most of all you love the fact that I won't stay and you know it. I'll never be yours, just as he won't ever really be mine. You'll yearn for me, for the fantasy you make of me, but you'll never capture me. And that is what you find most intriguing of all. That is why you find yourself chasing after me though even you know you shouldn't. I'm not any good for you."

His voice was even but she could hear the slight tone in it that betrayed how much he wanted her to change her mind. "It doesn't have to be this way. We don't have to play this game, you know. You don't have to chase a phantom and I don't have to love one. We don't have to hurt one another."

His words made her angry. She turned to face him, suddenly furious with him, furious at his refusal to understand and for making this harder than it needed to be. "You think that, don't you? You think I have a choice in the matter, as if I can choose what I am. I can't help who I am. Hurting people is what I do. That's why you are much better off without me. It is why I won't stay. I don't want to stay and see you die at my own hand."

He reached out a hand, as if to pull her closer, and she jerked backward, bumping up against the window. He let the hand drop to his side. His eyes grew soft and sad. "Zhara, you are better than you give yourself credit for being. You don't have to hurt people. You don't have to be hurt. You can open up and let yourself be loved for once."

She shook her head and pushed past him. She suddenly felt afraid. She needed to leave. Now.

"You don't understand. You'll never understand. I CAN'T! I CAN'T LOVE YOU! I don't know what that is! I don't know what it means!"

She was out the door and down the hall before she said the final words. "I don't know how to love you. I don't know how to love anyone. I don't know how to love."

She climbed on the back of her motorcycle, blinking away the tears that were threatening, not even bothering to put on her helmet. She didn't want to be safe. She didn't want to be secure. She didn't deserve it. She gunned the engine and sped off into the night without looking back, heading straight into the mouth of hell. She was headed straight for Damien.

~ ~

Damien's dark eyes locked onto hers when she walked in the door. He didn't say a word. He knew why she was there. Why waste words or breath talking about it?

He stood up and crossed the room with a panther-like grace that sent a shiver down her spine. He was everything she knew she shouldn't but couldn't help herself but want.

He didn't ask permission or wait for her consent to kiss her. He wasn't tender, polite, or gentle about it. She didn't want him to be. Tenderness, politeness, and gentleness were not things she needed or deserved.

She felt a surge of passion for him that left her breathless and eager for more. He was the drug she couldn't get enough of even though she knew it was no good for her. She would hate herself in the morning, but tonight she needed him, wanted him, and would allow him to have her in any way that he wanted her.

They were halfway to the bedroom, clothes strewn across the floor, when John's face broke through the fog of desire. John's voice calling her name, begging her to reconsider, pleading with her not to leave.

She froze in place, unable to move. Damien growled impatiently and swept her off her feet, carrying her into the bedroom and dumping her on the bed. She looked up at him and shook her head. "No. No more."

His face darkened and he scowled. "What are you playing at, Zhara?"

Her face flushed and she suddenly found herself ashamed of her nakedness. She grabbed the sheet from the foot of the bed and covered herself with it. "I'm not playing at anything. I just…don't want this. I've changed my mind."

Damien stared at her, his face inscrutable. "Who is he?"

Her eyes widened and she looked away. "I don't know what you mean."

Damien ripped the sheet out of her hands, exposing her. She covered herself with her hands as he leaned closer to her and hissed the question. "Who. Is. He?"

Damien's normally dark eyes were nearly black. His face was flushed red.

Something clicked inside her head and a sudden realization came over her. "You – you're jealous."

Damien pulled back as if she'd slapped him. She saw his jaw tighten and his hands flex. His eyes hardened and he stepped back from the bed. "Get. Out."

She felt a cold chill slide down the back of her spine. "Damien, I don't…"

He roared the words. "GET OUT!"

She slid out of his bed and gathered up her clothes, doing her best to put them on as quickly as he was throwing them at her. "GET OUT!"

She fled out the door and into the night, unsure of where to go. She couldn't face John, not after everything she'd done to him, and it was clear that Damien didn't want her there. Where was there to go when you weren't good enough for Heaven but Hell had just kicked you out?

She checked her watch. It was 11 at night. Purgatory wouldn't close for another couple of hours at least.

Chapter 2

Zhara stepped through the doors of Purgatory a half-hour later. The bar was crowded, the music was thumping, and the drinks were flowing. Mike's bald head gleamed in the light from behind the bar. Gabby, his twin sister, was weaving her way through, delivering drinks with the deftness of long practice, teasing some and swatting away the hands of others.

She made her way through the crowd and took a seat at the bar. Mike raised an eyebrow when he spotted her and nodded even as he finished pouring a drink and serving a customer. She waited patiently. He would come for her when he could. He always did.

"You're one of Damien's girls, aren't you?" The rough voice behind her was vaguely familiar.

She turned to find a tall, well-built stranger with his arms crossed in front of his chest staring her down. "Not tonight. Tonight, I'm nobody's girl."

A grin stretched across his face. He placed a hand on the bar next to her and leaned a little too close. "If Damien's through playing with you, you could always come play with me."

She crossed her arms in front of her chest and shook her head. Dark curls bounced around her face. "I don't feel like breaking any more toys tonight. Go find someone else to play with. I'm not in the mood for games."

A scowl settled across his face and a hint of red began to creep up his collar line. She rolled her eyes. This man just wasn't going to take no for an answer. She knew the type.

He seized hold of her arm and leaned into her, so close that she could smell the whiskey on his breath. "I said I want you to come play with me. Don't make me…"

His words cut off with a startled yelp. Zhara's knife blade gleamed in the light, just a hair's breadth from the man's groin. "I told you. I don't want to break any more toys tonight. Don't make me."

He let go of her arm and backed off. "No wonder Damien's done playing with you."

She didn't say a word. She just kept her knife in her hand and her eyes locked on his face until he returned to his seat.

"There you go again getting yourself into trouble. Zhara, Zhara, what have you been up to?"

She tucked the knife back into the strap at her thigh and turned around to greet Mike. "I don't get myself into trouble, Mike. Trouble just happens to find me."

He shook his head and winked. "It does seem to follow you wherever you go. I'll give you that much. What can I get you tonight?"

She winced. "Devil's Kiss, and Angel Tears."

Mike's grin disappeared. "Who broke your heart? Whose face am I going to need to go break?"

She shook her head and held up a hand. "Didn't. I broke my own. I messed it up. With both of them. On the same night."

Mike crossed his arms for a moment. "Promise me you're going to stay until close. I have GOT to hear that story."

She sighed. "I've got nowhere else to go. I'm not good enough for Heaven, and Hell doesn't want me there."

Mike didn't say anything. He just walked over and started pouring her drinks. He returned a few minutes later and set them down in front of her. "I'll be back later to collect the story. Let me know if you need anything else."

She contented herself with tossing back the Devil's Kiss first. The scotch seared the inside of her throat as it went down. A perfect tribute to Damien.

In the six years she'd known Damien, he'd never once said anything close to "I love you" or asked for her to be his alone. He'd certainly made it clear that he belonged to nobody and didn't want to belong to anybody.

Their relationship was undefined with no promises and no commitments. She'd been comfortable with that until she met John. She hadn't needed promises people couldn't keep or commitments they would only break later.

Damien's flare of jealousy tonight caught her off guard. It was unlike him. He'd never asked her before who she was with when she wasn't with him. He'd never seemed to care. But he did now. It confused her. His anger confused her.

But John was different. He said things and meant them. Around him, for the first time in her life, she found herself craving stability and permanence.

She'd always feared commitments. She'd feared being tied down, held in place, caged in a life too small for her. John made her want to stay in place.

He made her wonder what it would be like to be in a relationship that wasn't fluid but was solid and structured. To have a man say, and mean, that he would love you until the end of his days. To say those words to him in return. For once, commitment didn't seem like a cage but more like a safe house.

And that, even more than Damien's sudden bout of jealousy, confused her. She didn't know what had shifted in her, but something had changed. She wasn't the same woman she'd been when this began.

She didn't know what that meant, but what she did know was that the relationship she'd shared with Damien was not going to survive this change. She wasn't sure she was capable of making a lifelong commitment to anyone, and she knew she didn't have whatever it was that John needed for her to give him, but she wasn't satisfied with whatever passed for her relationship with Damien. It wasn't enough for her anymore.

She took a sip of the Angel Tears. Sweet and bitter at the same time. She lingered over this drink, not wanting to finish it. What she wanted was to go back to John. She knew she could go there right this instant and he would open the door for her and take her back in without a single question asked. He would open his arms and let her step into them and wrap them around her as if she'd never done anything to hurt him.

But she wouldn't let herself do that. She wasn't ready to be the woman he deserved to have in his arms and in his life. She didn't even know if she could be that woman. She frowned as she drank the last of her drink.

She didn't know if she could ever be that woman, but the question she needed to ask herself was, "Was she ready to try?" Could she change for John? Was that even possible for her?

She frowned. What if she tried and she failed? What if she tried to be who John wanted, needed, her to be and she couldn't be that? What if she hurt him even more because of her failure?

Mike appeared as she was asking herself the questions and collected her empties. "Last call if you want something, darlin'. It's getting close to closing time. Another Devil's Kiss for you? Or would you prefer another round of Angel Tears?"

She grimaced. No more Angel Tears. No more hurting John. No more Devil's Kisses, either. That bridge was burned. "Just a Jack and Coke this time. Tall."

Mike nodded. "Why don't you take a seat at one of the tables and I'll have Gabby bring it to you."

She slid off the bar stool and made her way through the thinning crowd to the table furthest in the back to wait for Gabby to deliver the drink. She didn't have long to wait.

Gabby threaded her way through and dropped off the Jack and Coke, along with a kiss on the top of Zhara's head. "How's my favorite little sister doing tonight? Mike said you were having some man troubles?"

Zhara sighed and shrugged. "The trouble's not with the men. It's with me."

Gabby frowned and picked her tray back up off the table. "Stay right there. I'll be back in about 30 minutes and we can talk about it."

Zhara watched Gabby work her way through the crowd and sipped her drink, watching as the place began to empty out after drinks were delivered and tabs were settled.

Forty-five minutes later, Gabby swooped in and took a seat beside her. "What a night! This place was crawling with people. Great for tips, but not so great for the feet. So tell me about your troubles, Z. I'm all ears."

Zhara sighed and told her about the evening with John and then the way things ended with Damien. Gabby's brows rose in surprise when she got to the part about Damien tossing her out when she wouldn't talk about John with him. "Wait. Wait. Did I hear you right? Damien was upset about you being with another guy? That guy changes women like some guys change socks!"

She frowned. It was true. Damien was a magnet for women. He drew them in and then discarded them so often it was hard to keep track.

She was one of the only women he'd kept around, but she suspected that was largely because she'd never made a big deal of their relationship or pushed for more than he'd been willing to give her. "He was not upset. He was furious. Angry enough to throw my clothes at me and toss me out. I still don't understand it."

Gabby grinned. "What's to understand? You got to him. The untouchable heart has been touched by you."

Zhara studied the glass in her hand. "I don't know about that. I just know he wanted me out."

Gabby put a hand on Zhara's arm. "Sounds like you had quite the evening. I'm sure Damien will come back to you when he's had a chance to cool off. If you want him to come back to you, that is."

She cocked her head to the side slightly and raised an eyebrow. "Do you? Want Damien to come back to you?"

That was a question Zhara hadn't asked herself yet. "Honestly? If I had to answer that question, I'd say I don't know. I always thought that I couldn't live if Damien weren't part of my life anymore, but right now, I think I'm just…done. I'm done with being one of many. I am done with competing for a man's attention. I want a man who looks at me and sees me, wants me, and loves me. I don't think Damien can give that to me."

Gabby clapped her hands slowly and reached over to hug Zhara. "Congratulations. I've been waiting for you to decide that for a while now. I couldn't stop you from chasing after Damien, and I'll grant you that the man is hotter than a $2 pistol, but I am glad you are ready for something better than being one of his girls. You deserve more."

Zhara felt tears forming and closed her eyes to shut them down. "Do I? Why don't I feel like I'm worth more? What if I don't have what it takes?"

Gabby wrapped her arms even tighter around Zhara. "You have it. You just need to find it. And you will."

Chapter 3

Damien paced the floors of his living room. Damn that woman to hell and back again. Damn her. Damn her for the fact that he wanted her, now. Damn her for the fact that he didn't WANT to want her.

She was the one constant in his life, like the northern star in the sky above, and he hated her for it. He hated her for the power she held over him without any effort or attempt on her part. No matter how many other women came and went, he couldn't let go of her. He'd tried, but she was like the ocean in that regard. She kept pulling him back to her.

Zhara was the one weakness he had, and weakness was a dangerous thing. Weakness left you open and vulnerable and made you easy to hurt. No woman was ever going to hurt him again. He'd sworn that long before he met her.

Now here he was, six years later, hating himself for letting her get close to him. Hating himself for letting her hurt him. Hating himself for loving her. Hating himself for letting her walk out that door.

He sat on the couch and put his head in his hands. He'd never minded the other men in her life before. Why did it matter? She would come back to him. He'd known it, always. She would find her way back to him just as surely as he would find his way back to her.

But not this time. This time was different. This man was different. He held a power over her that Damien did not understand. But he'd seen it in her eyes. The way she'd pulled back from him. The way she'd suddenly changed her mind. She'd hidden him from Damien, protected him. He meant something to her in a way the other men hadn't.

He stood back up and paced again, feeling like a tiger in a cage. He wanted to go and find her. To possess her. Make her his again. To kiss her until every trace of that other man was erased from her mind and her soul.

Instead, he got up and walked over to the refrigerator, pulled out a beer from the refrigerator, and popped the top. He drank it and then threw the glass bottle as hard as he could across the room, feeling a sense of satisfaction when it exploded against the wall. Glass shards spread everywhere.

He glanced over at his phone and thought for a moment about calling her number. But what would he say to her? He wasn't about to beg her to come back. He didn't want her to know how badly he wanted her, needed her. Besides, it wouldn't change anything. She wouldn't come. She was probably with that man even now.

A thunderous rage filled him at the thought of his rival. Whoever he was, wherever he was, he would find him, and he would make him pay. Nobody would take what belonged to him. Nobody. And Zhara did belong to him, as much as he belonged to her. He couldn't escape her, and he wouldn't let her escape him. She ought to know that by now.

He threw on his jacket and stepped out into the cool night air. It was time to go get what was his.

~ ~

John watched Zhara walk out the door. He didn't try to stop her. She would come back when she was ready, or she wasn't the woman he thought she was.

He heard the engine of her motorcycle roar to life and listened as she sped away. He knew where she was headed. The same place she always headed when she got scared and things got a little too good, a little too real, for her. Straight to Damien.

It was as if she needed to punish herself for feeling happy, to remind herself of just how little she believed she was worth, by going straight to the man who was most likely to use her up and leave her broken. He wished he could understand what she saw in Damien. The man seemed to do nothing but hurt her.

He hated having to compete with him for Zhara's heart. She deserved the best and that's all he wanted to give her, but no matter how much love he poured into her, she just couldn't seem to hold onto it. In fact, the more love he tried to give her, the more skittish she became.

She wasn't entirely wrong when she'd told him that he loved her and she didn't even have to do anything to earn it. He'd loved her from the moment he met her. She was fire and light, passion and brilliance. He was absolutely enchanted with her.

It wasn't her body that drew him to her, although she was an incredibly attractive woman, but her heart and the way her mind worked. He'd never met another woman like her and he knew that he never would. She was as unique as any masterpiece artwork.

He wanted her to just open up and let him in, but earning her trust wasn't easy. He could tell she'd been hurt, and often, by the men in her life. He didn't want to be one more of those. He sighed and poured himself a glass of wine before heading over to the piano and sitting down to play.

Music was the thing that drew Zahra to him, and music was what would soothe his soul now. He allowed all the hurt and the frustration and the struggle to pour out of him and into the keyboard. He played for her, even though he knew she couldn't hear it, and allowed everything he was feeling to express itself in the notes. He played until there was nothing left but peace in his soul.

She would come back to him when she was ready. He was certain of it. And when she was ready to come back, the door – and his heart – would be open and waiting to receive her.

~ ~

"Where is she?"

Mike looked up from where he was wiping down the bar and frowned as he spotted Damien. "What do you want?"

Damien stared at Mike without flinching. "Where is Zhara?"

Mike stopped wiping the bar and locked eyes with Damien. "What's it to you? Last time I checked, she didn't belong to you."

Damien's scowl deepened. "Tell me where she is. Now."

Mike stepped back and crossed his arms over his chest. "If she wanted you to know where she was, she would have told you herself. She's a big girl and she's perfectly capable of letting you know if she wanted you to know."

Damien's jaw clenched. "I know she's here. I saw her bike in the parking lot. You tell her I want to talk to her. Tell her it's not over."

Mike put both hands on the counter and leaned forward. "For six years, I've watched you put that girl through hell. I couldn't stop her from running back to you anytime you crooked your finger her direction. God knows, I tried. She wouldn't listen. She's finally deciding enough is enough, and I'll be damned if I'm going to help you destroy her again."

Damien's fists curled. Mike willed him to go ahead and throw a punch. Just one was all he needed. But the man backed off. He turned on his heel and headed toward the door.

"This isn't over. You tell her I'm going to find her. I don't care where I have to go or what I have to do, but I'm going to find her."

Mike crossed his arms over his chest and waited until he heard Damien's motorcycle start up before he called upstairs to alert Gabby to the situation.

~ ~

"Six years and it turns out all I had to do to get Damien to finally decide he wanted me was to walk away? Figures."

Zhara's voice held a note of undisguised contempt. Gabby wasn't sure whether the contempt was for Damien, for Zhara, or for the both of them.

"You're not considering going back to him, are you?"

Zhara shook her head.

"No. Is it sad that I finally get what I always thought I wanted – for Damien to show me that he gave a damn about me – and all it does is leave me cold? He had six years to decide that he loved me and wanted me to be with him. He had all the chances in the world to show me that he cared. I finally have a man in my life who wants me and who cares about me. He isn't going to take that away from me."

Gabby put an arm around Zhara's shoulders.

"You're welcome to stay with us as long as you need to. I don't think it's a good idea for you to go back home, though. I don't know what he plans to do once he does find you, but I doubt it's going to be good. Mike said he looked like he was ready to breathe fire."

Zhara sighed and shrugged.

"I'm sure if I just lay low for a week or so, he'll forget all about me in some other woman's bed. It's what he usually does. We fight, he gets mad, he sleeps with someone else until he's not mad anymore. For Damien, sex is the cure for everything that ails you."

Gabby hugged her.

"Well, here's to new beginnings with a man who doesn't use you as therapy. You do know you're going to have to introduce us to John, right? I can't let my little sister go running off with some man I've never met."

Zhara blushed.

"Last time I brought home a man, you didn't approve."

Gabby snorted.

"Last time you brought home Damien. My own personal feelings about him aside, the man was 22 and you were 16. Are you surprised I didn't approve?"

Zhara sighed.

"No, not really. I just wish I'd listened. Might have saved us all some heartache."

Gabby ruffled her hair and kissed the top of it.

"Yeah, well, you're listening now. That's all that matters."

Zhara frowned slightly and looked out the window.

"Let's hope so."

Chapter 4

"Was he there again tonight, Mike? Be honest with me."

Mike threw an arm around Zhara and gave her a side hug. "It's not a big deal. He's not causing any trouble. All he does is drink and stare. I wish all my customers were that well behaved."

Her forehead crinkled with concern. "I should just go over there and see him. Talk to him. Tell him I'm not coming back."

He let go of her and took a swig of his beer. "Absolutely not. He'll give up eventually."

She frowned. "I don't think so. It's been a week already and he's not given up yet."

He shrugged. "You're a grown woman and I can't tell you what to do, but I think you going over there is just going to encourage him. I don't think it's going to stop him."

She leaned against him. "Why couldn't he have been this interested in me when I actually wanted him and cared about him? Why does he have to wait until now?"

He leaned back and sighed. "It's a matter of pride for him. It's a matter of honor. You're rejecting him. The minute you take him back in is the minute he'll stop fighting for you and stop caring. Don't feed the monster. Don't give him what he wants."

She put a finger to her mouth and started chewing a fingernail. "I just don't get him. I don't. He doesn't really care about me, so why can't he just let me go? Why does he have to go full on stalker mode the minute I say I'm done?"

He took another sip of his beer. "He's always been the one in control. He's always been the one to end things. I'm sure this all feels very new to him to have the shoe be on the other foot. Some guys just don't handle rejection well."

She stood up and walked over to the window. "I can't stand this. I can't stand waiting for him to do whatever it is he's going to do. I can't stand playing a game of endless hide-and-go-seek. That's just not who I am. I know you don't want me to, but I'm going over there and I'm going to tell him to back off."

He closed his eyes and leaned his head back on the couch. "Zhara, for the love of all that's good and holy, don't do it. I don't honestly know what's gotten into him. I get that you don't want to stay cooped up in the apartment. Maybe you should think about getting out of town for a while. Just take a road trip. Go somewhere, anywhere, just not here. Come back in a few weeks when he's had time to find another hobby."

She didn't say anything. She didn't move. She just kept staring out the window. He might have thought she hadn't heard him but he knew her well enough to know it meant she was thinking through her options. He kept quiet and gave her the space to think.

"Maybe. Maybe that's exactly what I need to do." Her voice sounded distant, almost like she wasn't really talking to him. He felt a chill run down his spine but he put a smile on his face. "Where do you think you'll head? There's plenty of places with pretty views and scenic routes."

She stood there a few minutes longer and then turned around as if she'd made some decision. She smiled at him, gave him a hug, grabbed her bag, and her keys. "I'm not sure yet. I'll call you when I get there."

He stopped her and locked eyes with her. "Promise? You're not going to do something reckless are you?"

She looked him in the eyes. "Nope. Nothing reckless. I promise I'll call you when I get there."

He couldn't help but feel like she wasn't telling him something. He frowned, but he didn't want to outright accuse her of lying to him when he had no proof. Instead, he hugged her close. "I'll have my phone on. If you need me, you know how to reach me."

She returned the hug and then stepped away, turned on her heel, and walked out the door. "Thanks for everything. I won't forget to call. I promise. Tell Gabby I'll talk to her soon."

~ ~

Zhara climbed on her bike for the first time since the night she'd been kicked out by Damien. It felt good to hear the engine roar to life. She wasn't sure where she was going but she was happy to be doing something with her life rather than sitting and waiting for life to happen to her.

She turned on the high beams and pulled out onto the open high-way, gunning it as soon as she crossed the county line. There were fewer cops out here.

The night air felt amazing. It was cool and refreshing. For the first time, she felt peace settle into her soul. Out here there was no Damien and no John. It was just her, the motorcycle, and the road. And that was all she needed for the moment.

She found the small trail that led to the cabin and turned off the highway, switching the bike to a lower gear. It was dark and the road was rough. It hadn't been traveled in some years. Not since her grandfather's death.

She pulled up to the cabin and sat there, allowing the headlights to bathe it in the warm light. She hesitated. Coming out to the cabin and reconnecting with her roots had felt right when she'd thought about doing it three hours ago in the safety and comfort of Mike and Gabby's apartment. Now it just felt like trespassing. The cabin belonged to her by law, but she wasn't sure the ghosts that haunted it were ready to give it up.

As if to confirm her suspicions, she watched as the front port swing began to sway back and forth just as the wind died down. She felt goosebumps prickle on her arms despite the thick leather jacket she was wearing and the hair on the back of her neck raise.

She took off her helmet and hung it on the front bar of the bike before dismounting. She gathered up her courage and her flashlight, forcing herself to walk up the steps to the cabin's front door. "It's just me, Grandpa. It's just your Shining Flower."

The porch swing stilled and came to a stop. She half expected the door to open on its own, but it remained fastened tight. Her hands shook as she pulled open the keys and unlocked the door.

Moonlight spilled through a window in the back, giving her just enough light to see by. She pulled out her lighter and took down the oil lantern from its place beside the door.

Grandpa didn't believe in electricity or indoor plumbing. He'd never bothered to install either. "Live simple, girl. You'll be happier that way. Fewer bills to pay and less things to worry about. Mark my word."

It took a few tries before the wick caught and the lantern began giving off a steady glow. She stood in the doorway looking around. Everything was exactly the way she remembered it, as if time itself hadn't touched the place since the day the people from child services had taken her away.

The cabin felt smaller than she remembered. She supposed that was because she'd gotten taller and grown older. But it was still recognizably his cabin. Everything was neat, tidy, and precisely where it was meant to be. Just the way he'd left it.

She crossed the floor to the short ladder leading up to the sleeping loft and climbed up, holding the lantern to light her way. The bed was still carefully made, although there was a layer of thick dust covering it now.

She crawled up into the bed area and opened the small window to let in the fresh breezes. She carefully bundled up the top blanket, careful to disturb as little of the dust as possible, and headed back down the stairs to the front porch to shake it out. "I wish you were here, Grandpa. You'd know the right thing to say. You'd know what I'm supposed to do. I sure don't. Everything just seems so complicated right now. I love John, but I don't think I'm any good for him. I think if I'm with him, I'll just hurt him."

She paused to wipe a bead of sweat from her brow. "And Damien? Well, I used to think I loved him. But now, I think he's…I don't know. I guess he's comfortable. Familiar. I know what to expect with him even if what I can expect with him is to get hurt. Is it sad that the safer of the two men is the one who scares me the most?"

The wind picked up right then and captured a corner of the blanket, tugging it out of her hands and shaking the blanket hard enough so that the dust flew up in a cloud before settling back down. She buried her face in the blanket. It now smelled fresher and cleaner.

She climbed back up into the loft and lay down, being careful to blow the lantern out before she did. A bone-deep tired tugged at her eyelids and she found herself falling deep asleep in no time. The front porch swing began to rock back and forth in a steady motion.

Chapter 5

In the two weeks since Zhara walked out of his door something inside John began dying. He'd played until his fingers bled and couldn't find peace in the music anymore. Everything felt off. Everything felt wrong. There was always something missing in it, and that something was Zhara.

The problem was that he didn't want to corner her or pressure her. He knew that would only be a recipe that would make her run away from him. She would see in it the same kind of behavior she'd seen out of Damien.

He had a rule to treat people, including and maybe especially Zhara, like a beloved cat. He petted them when they were ready to be petted. He snuggled them when they were ready to be snuggled. He let them go when they were ready to be let go. He didn't take it personally. He just gave them their space.

For the most part, it worked. It kept him sane and them free. But right now, he needed to see her. He needed to at least know that she was okay. He wanted her to know that his door would always be open to her whenever she was ready.

But he didn't know where to begin looking for her. She'd always come to him. She'd never allowed him to come to her. It was almost like she was ashamed of her past and afraid of having him see it.

He sat on the couch with a glass of wine and tried to relax his mind, calling up memories of past conversations they'd had to gather clues about where he might go to find her. He couldn't think of anything that seemed particularly striking. Nothing that you could type into a browser search and get concrete answers.

He was getting frustrated. Normally, his solution to getting the attention of someone who escaped him and he wanted to draw back to him was to find their particular brand of "tuna" and set it out like bait. It was a trick that worked more often than not. But that trick only worked if the "cat" in question was close enough at hand to catch the scent. He had a gut feeling that Zhara was straying a little too far for it to work.

The obvious place to go to check on Zhara was a visit to Damien's. However, he seriously doubted that confrontation would go well.

What was he going to say to the man? "Hello. About Zhara. Do you happen to know where I could find her? I'm madly in love with her and trying to entice her to leave you for good. Would you be so kind as to tell me where she might be?"

Yeah. No. There was no way that conversation was going to end in civil discourse. From everything that Zhara told her about Damien, he was a man very much ruled by his emotions. And when it came to Zhara, those emotions were very unstable.

He glanced over at the coffee table and spotted a matchbook he knew wasn't his own. The name on it was Purgatory. It had an address. It sounded like the exact kind of place that Zhara would frequent. In fact, he was fairly certain this belonged to her. He felt a tiny bit of hope spring to life.

~ ~

Damien settled into his usual spot in the back corner to watch for Zhara. She couldn't stay in hiding forever. One of these days she was going to come out and when she did, he would be ready. She would be coming home with him that night whether she wanted to or not.

A tall, thin, elegantly dressed man made his way through the crowd that night and stopped at the bar. It was hard not to notice him. He looked so out of place. Damien's curiosity was immediately roused. Who was this man and what was he doing in a place like this?

Instinct told him to draw closer. He listened. He stood up and made his way through the crowd. He got close enough that he could hear a bit of the conversation, the only bit that mattered to him.

"Zhara."

Damien dissolved into the crowd, hopeful that Mike would be too distracted by the stranger to notice him, and walked back to his table. He tossed a few dollars on his table to cover his drinks and slipped out the door, waiting for that man to leave. If this man had answers about where Zhara was and what she was doing, he was going to get them. He stepped back out into the cool night air and settled in to wait.

He didn't have long to wait. The man's face was fallen and his shoulders were slightly stooped. Based on his body posture and facial expression, Damien guessed his conversation with Mike hadn't proven any more fruitful than the conversations Damien had with him.

Still, more information was always helpful. He wanted to know what the stranger knew about her. "You looking for Zhara?"

The man stopped in his tracks and looked over at Damien. His eyebrows shot straight up to his hairline, which was neatly and tidily trimmed. "As a matter of fact, I am. Do you know her?"

Damien stepped forward and crossed his arms in front of his chest. He gave the man a slow, lazy grin. "You could say that. I've known her for quite some time."

The man's crystal blue eyes seemed to peer straight into Damien's soul. Damien shifted uncomfortably and frowned. He asked the man a question, trying to regain control over the conversation. "How do you know her?"

The man hesitated a moment and his eyes took in the apparently empty parking lot. A frown flitted across his face before he forced a smile onto it and then looked back at Damien. "She attended a concert of mine. I was hoping to invite her to the next one."

Damien scowled suddenly. "Were you? I don't know if she mentioned this to you or not, but she's with someone already."

The man cocked his head to the side and the smile left his face. A resolve hardened his features. His reply was polite but there was an undercurrent of contempt beneath the words. "Is she? I would think she would have mentioned it. Perhaps the young lady isn't aware she's with someone."

Damien took a menacing step forward, drawing himself up to his full height. He expected the man to draw back. It was what most men did in the face of Damien's obvious size and power. Instead, the man stood his ground and held his eyes. There was no fear in them, just a simple determination.

Damien found himself uneasy. The thousand and one things he'd imagined himself doing if he ever found the man who'd tried to take

Zhara from him didn't seem to fit in this moment. He clenched his fists reflexively. The man's voice broke through Damien's confusion. "Where are my manners? We haven't been properly introduced. I'm John. I'm fairly certain that your name is Damien. If I'm right, let me offer you some sage advice, from one man to another. Stay away from Zhara. Give her time to think, time to breathe, and time to decide for herself what she wants. If she wants you, she will seek you out. If she doesn't, trying to force her to be with you will only result in the two of you getting hurt."

With that, the man walked off to his car as if nothing important had just happened. Damien was too stunned to follow after him.

~ ~

Damien walked back into the bar after watching the man's car drive off and resumed his seat at his table. It was time for a new plan. Clearly, Zhara wasn't with another man and she wasn't coming here. He needed to think, and thinking rhymed with drinking.

Gabby came by right before closing time. "Last call. You want anything else?"

He smirked and crossed his arms in front of his chest. "Nothing that's on the menu."

Her grey eyes locked onto his and she leaned forward slightly. A smile slowly stretched across her face. Her voice was sultry and smooth. "Do you know what I think you want?"

He raised an eyebrow and held her gaze. "No. What?"

She narrowed her eyes. "A good ass whooping, that's what I think you want, Damien McKnight."

She leaned over just a little closer and hissed into his ear. "And if you don't stay away from my little sister, that's exactly what I'm going to make sure you get."

Damien held her gaze before letting his eyes sweep down her generous curves. "Are you offering? Because I just might be willing to let you try if you're the one delivering my ass whooping."

Gabby turned away from him without a single word and headed to the next table. A thought came to mind. Maybe Gabby was the new plan. Threatening Zhara just made her go into hiding. Chasing her just made her run. But if Gabby were in danger, he had no doubt that Zhara would find her way to him in record time.

He stood up and headed out the door. He was going to need time to prepare the right cage for this pretty little kitty. He whistled as he walked. He felt better than he had since Zhara walked out the door. This was going to be fun.

Chapter 6

"Your mother would still be with us if that bastard hadn't taken her away from us."

Zhara sat on the porch swing beside her grandfather. Her feet dangled in the air. She was still too little to touch the ground. The old man looked down at Zhara and his face softened.

He hugged her close. "You look just like her."

Zhara snuggled into her grandfather. His familiar warmth was a comfort to her. She loved the way he smelled of wood smoke and fresh turned earth. He was solid and sturdy in a world that seemed to constantly fall apart beneath her. "I'll never let anything happen to you, Zhara girl. That's a promise" He kissed her on the top of her head and then stood up, reaching for her hand and helping her off the swing. "First things first, we are heading into town. It's time for spring planting and that means seed picking time. What are we going to plant this year, my shining flower?"

Zhara giggled and looked up at her grandfather. "Can we plant pumpkins?"

If there was one thing she loved, it was pumpkins. She loved her grandmother's pumpkin muffins and pumpkin bread. She loved pumpkin carving and visiting the pumpkin patches each fall. She dreamed of growing great big pumpkins like she'd seen at the fair last year.

Her grandfather looked down at her and there was a slight frown on her face. She wondered if he was going to tell her no. "We'll try, but I don't know if this climate can handle pumpkins. But I promise we'll try."

They drove to the feed store and stepped inside. Zhara gasped aloud as she spotted what appeared to be a large bear sleeping by the counter. She looked to her grandfather and grasped his hand. He smiled and patted her hand. "Don't mind Bear. He's friendly."

The "bear" raised his head and stood up, padding softly over toward Zhara. She realized it was not a bear but a very large black and brown dog. He sniffed her first and then licked her face gently. She giggled at the feel of it and reached out a hand to pet him. He was almost as tall as she was.

They picked out the seeds next, and Zhara got her scoop of pumpkin seeds from the bin. They walked up to the counter to pay and Bear came up to join them. She rested her head on his for a moment and slid her arms around him. He seemed happy to have her there.

There were three more stops before they headed home that day. The first was to the grocery store to pick out some flowers. Her grandpa let her choose a set for Grandma and a set for her mom. The next stop was to the cemetery. As often as they came to town, they made this trip.

They made their way to the family plot. Her grandfather took off his hat as he got closer and knelt right in front of her grandmother's tombstone, placing the flowers at the base. "Ellie, I brought Zhara with me today. She's doing well, I think. She's turning ten already. I wish you were here to see it. She looks just like our Caroline."

He reached out a hand and caressed the tombstone with all the tenderness he'd once caressed the cheek of his wife. "Hard to believe you've been gone nearly three years already. I sure do miss you. I never expected to be raising a little girl all by myself. But, I know God called you home for a reason. Even if I don't really understand. You rest well. I'll be joining you just as soon as I finish up raising Zhara. She needs me, you see? I can't let happen to her what happened to Caroline."

He reached over and kissed the stone. Zhara waited patiently, her mother's bouquet in her grip.

He stepped back from her grandmother's gravestone and gathered Zhara's hand in his. "Time to say hello to your mother, Zhara. Why don't you go ahead and place the flowers there on her tombstone?"

Zhara reluctantly did as her grandfather asked. She didn't like visiting. She barely remembered her mother anymore. It felt awkward saying hello to someone she didn't really know. "Hi, Mom. Grandpa and I bought seeds today. He let me buy some pumpkin seeds. He told me he wasn't sure if they would grow, but I think they will. Maybe next time we come, I'll have a pumpkin to give you."

That was all she could think of to say, so she stepped back and let her grandfather step forward to have his say. "Oh, my baby. My Caroline. You have no idea how much I miss you. Your daughter's getting bigger by the minute. I'm keeping her safe for you. Don't you worry. I won't let that bastard do to her what he did to you."

Zhara knew "that bastard" was her father. Nobody would tell her what he'd done. Just that it was evil and wicked and that it was bad enough that you shouldn't even talk about it.

Her grandfather reached out a hand and caressed the stone. "She looks just like you. Just as pretty as a peach. And smart as a whip, let me tell you. Nothing gets by her. You'd be proud of her." He lingered a moment, kissed the gravestone, and then scooped Zhara up in a hug before setting her down on her feet. "Nobody's ever going to hurt you the way they hurt my Caroline, Zhara. Nobody. That's a promise."

Zhara smiled up at her grandpa. She was sure he meant it, too. "Next stop: Buttered Pecan Ice Cream. You ready?"

Zhara grinned and nodded. It was their thing together. When Grandma had been alive, they'd snuck it into the house and eaten it together late at night in the kitchen so Grandma didn't know. No visit to town was ever complete without a carton of Buttered Pecan Ice Cream to take home with them.

Now, it was their way of remembering Grandma. It was a shared indulgence that brought them closer together.

~ ~

Zhara woke with a taste for Buttered Pecan Ice Cream in her mouth and a longing for her grandfather that overwhelmed her. She'd never gotten to see the pumpkins ripen that year. He died of a heart attack brought on by heat stroke that summer.

She'd found him sitting underneath one of the apple trees he'd planted. His eyes were closed and he looked peaceful, as if he were just taking a nap. She could remember screaming and crying the moment she figured out he was gone and she was all alone.

That was the end of her life on the family farm. The end of stability and security. Child protective services had arrived a few days later to take her away. She'd discovered last year that her grandfather had placed the farm into a trust until her twenty first birthday. Even after she got the letter, though, she hadn't found the courage to visit. There were too many memories here.

However, with Damien stalking her, now had seemed like a perfect time to come back and settle things. She still didn't know what she was going to do with the place. Selling it seemed wrong, somehow, but she couldn't see herself living here permanently. There would be time for those decisions later.

She climbed down the ladder and headed for her bike to retrieve her bag. She'd forgotten to call Mike last night. He was bound to be worried by now. She just hoped she had enough power left in her phone to make the call.

The phone didn't pick up when she called. She let it ring through to voice mail. "Mike, this is Zhara. Just wanted to let you know I've arrived. I don't have much juice left so I may not be able to call again, but I want you to know I'm safe. I'll text you the address in case it's an emergency."

She sent the text message and then put the phone back in her bag and carted the whole thing into the house. She put her hands on her hips and looked around at the cabin. There was a lot of work to be done if she was going to stay here for any length of time.

There was water to be brought in from the well, wood to be stocked for the stove, and food to be gathered. It was the first part of fall already, so the berry bushes should be bursting with fruit.

"Well, Grandpa. It's just you and me now. What do you think I should do first?"

Her stomach growled quite loudly. That answered that question. Food first. Chores later. She slid on a pair of jeans and grabbed the berry picking bucket from its place in the shed. Grandpa was the kind of man who'd had a place for everything and everything definitely had its place. There was a comfort in knowing that, at least, hadn't changed.

Chapter 7

"She left us, Damien. That cold-hearted bitch just up and left us. That's what happens when you love a woman. They leave you. Women are the devil. Don't ever let them get close to you. All they ever do is cause you pain."

Damien struggled to hide the tears from his father. It would only earn him another beating. He missed his mother with an ache that just wouldn't stop. He didn't understand why she'd left him. She hadn't even stopped to say goodbye. She'd just left, as if he didn't matter.

At first, he'd refused to sleep at night. He kept hoping she would walk back through the door with that beautiful smile on her face, scoop him up in her arms like she always had, and make him feel safe again. But night after night passed and she didn't come back home. She didn't even call.

His father caught him crying himself to sleep one night, bawling for his mother, and yanked him out of the bed so hard it made his arm hurt.

He'd bent Damien over the bed, whipped off his leather belt, and began beating Damien. "You don't cry for that bitch anymore, you hear me, boy?"

Crack! "You don't cry for her."

Crack! "She doesn't deserve it."

Crack! "She's never"

Crack! "coming"

Crack! "back"

Crack "and you better just get used to it."

~ ~

Damien woke up in a cold sweat. He could still smell the beer on his father's breath and feel the leather belt as it whipped across his skin. He hadn't thought of the old man in years.

He slid out of bed and grabbed his jeans from the chair, tossing them on before stepping into the kitchen. He grabbed a beer out of the refrigerator and washed the taste of fear out of his mouth. His father was never, ever going to hit him again and no bitch was going to leave him ever again, either.

He picked up the phone and called an old friend. For the work he was about to do, he needed some place quiet and isolated. Some place nobody was likely to find him or interrupt him. "Tank. How you been, buddy?"

Tank's voice sounded skeptical. "Damien. Long time no hear. What can I do for you?"

Damien let a slow grin creep across his face. "You still got the keys to that old underground bunker at the abandoned military base?"

Tank paused. "Yeah. I got 'em. Why?"

Damien took a breath. "I've got this girl, see, and she really wants to see it. She kind of has a...thing...for places like that if you know what I mean. Just need to borrow it for a little while."

Tank chuckled. "You and your women. They just can't seem to get enough of you. Alright. You can borrow 'em. But I need em back next Wednesday. Boss is coming to town and I don't want him to know I've lent them out."

Damien grinned. "Not to worry. I'll make sure they're in your hands by Tuesday night."

An hour later, Damien was speeding out toward Tank's place to pick up the keys. Now that he had the keys to the cage, it was time to lure the kitty into it.

~ ~

"Last round, gentlemen! What can I get for you?" Gabby stopped by a table of off-duty marines and flashed them her best smile. She took their orders and then made her way back to the bar to fill up her tray with another round.

"Damien still sulking in his corner?" Mike's question caught Gabby off-guard. She'd gotten used to having Damien here every night and had, for the first time, forgotten him.

She shrugged briefly. "As long as he doesn't cause me trouble, I don't honestly care. Let him sulk. You heard from Zhara?"

Mike gave her a quick smile. "She sent me a text this morning with the address, but she said her cell service is low. I doubt we'll hear from her much. It's just as well. I miss having her here, but I worry less now that she's out of town."

Gabby nodded and sighed. "Maybe we can go visit her on Sunday when the bar's closed."

Mike grinned. "I bet she'd love that. Let's do it. It'll be nice to have a break from the crowd for a little bit."

Gabby swung back through the crowd one last time, delivering the drinks to their respective tables. She hesitated for a moment before stopping by Damien's table to check on him.

He had his hands locked behind his head and his chair tilted back. He gave her a smug grin as she made her approach and looked her up and down. "Come by to take my order? It's about time. I've been mighty thirsty for far too long."

She shook her head in disgust and put a hand on her hip. "I've had better lines from gumball machines. You're losing your touch. If that's the best you can do, you're going to be thirsty for a mighty long time. If you don't have a drink order to give me, I've got other customers to tend.

Damien tossed some money her direction. "That should cover my tab. Thanks for the service, Gabby. It's been great."

She snatched the money off the table and walked off in the direction of the bar. An hour later she began making the rounds again, letting the last of her customers know it was time to go. She stopped by Damien's table first.

"Still here? Sorry to break it to you, but it's closing time. You can come back and harass me some more tomorrow, but you're done for tonight."

He stood up, winked at her, and left without a word. She gritted her teeth as she watched him go. She was getting tired of him hanging around.

She and Mike spent the better part of an hour cleaning up after everyone was gone. She gathered up the garbage and headed out the backdoor to throw it into the dumpster. She was on her way back inside when she felt a hand clamp around her mouth and her face being covered with a cloth. An arm grabbed her around the middle and lifted her up off the ground.

A familiar voice chuckled. "No use struggling, Kitten. Take a few nice deep breathes and go to sleep. We're going to go for a ride, just you and me. It's high time we spent some quality time together."

She fought to free herself but it was no use. She felt herself growing dizzy and her eyes growing heavy. And then there was nothing but black.

~ ~

"Gabby? Did you fall into the dumpster? What's taking so long?" Mike headed toward the back only to find the door still open and his sister nowhere in sight. He felt his stomach drop. He grabbed the flashlight by the door and stepped outside.

He examined the ground, looking for clues as to what happened. He had a feeling he knew the answer, but he didn't want to accuse anyone until he was sure.

There was Gabby's smaller footprint making its way over to the garbage dump and then a much larger, booted print coming up behind hers. Her footprints disappeared after that.

He had a strong feeling he knew exactly whose boot prints those were. Damien. Damn the man. He'd caused enough trouble in their lives, but Mike hadn't suspected he would go this far.

He called the police to report his sister missing. They promised to go by Damien's house, but that was all they could do until she'd been missing at least 72 hours. In Damien's current state of unpredictability, Mike didn't know if Gabby had 24 hours, let alone 72.

It was time to talk to the one person who knew Damien better than anyone. He hated to disturb Zhara in her mountain retreat, but he was going to need her help if he was going to free Gabby.

~ ~

He nearly missed the small turn-off to the cabin but managed to find his way up to the cabin despite the darkness. He pounded on the door of the cabin until Zhara answered. She looked warn out and her dark hair was a mess.

Her eyes lit up on seeing him before worry took its place. "You wouldn't come out at this hour of the night for good news, would you, Mike?"

He shook his head. "I wish it were. It's Gabby. I think Damien's taken her."

She opened the door and let him inside. "Oh, my God. I knew Damien was dangerous but I never, I swear to you, I never thought he would do something like this."

Tears were forming in her eyes and Mike spoke the words he knew she needed to hear. "I know you didn't, Z. I know you'd never do anything to hurt Gabby. And that's why I'm here. I need your help to find her."

Zhara's jaw clenched and she nodded. "I'll do whatever you can. You know I will. I'd go to hell and back again if that is what it would take to save Gabby. What do you need me to do?"

Mike looked down at his hands. He knew that what he was about to ask Zhara to do was going to put her in immediate danger. But it was the only way to keep his sister safe.

He looked back up at Zhara. "I need you to come back to my place and make a phone call for me. Can you do that?"

Zhara nodded. "Give me a few minutes to get my things together and I'll be right on your tail."

Chapter 8

Gabby blinked and opened her eyes to darkness. She started to move and realized her hands were trapped. So were her legs. She tried to scream but something dry was stuffed in her mouth. Damien.

As if just thinking his name had summoned his presence, she heard footsteps on a concrete floor followed by a chuckle and felt a finger caress her cheek. She flinched away and heard him laugh.

"You ought to be nicer to me. Down here, I'm your only friend. Nobody knows where you are. If I were to leave, it could be months or even years before somebody finds you. It'd be a shame, too. Such a pretty girl like you to turn up dead in a place like this."

She could smell whiskey on his breath and wondered just how much he'd had to drink. "Of course, I don't really want you. You've got some mighty fine curves, but it's not you I'm after. It's your little sister. Bitch left me. But she'll come back to me quick enough once she knows I've got you. She loves you."

He paused and she felt her hair being played with. She resisted the urge to pull back. He was right. Wherever she was, he was her only way out. Nobody else knew where she was.

"Everybody loves you. You and your brother. Even in high school, they all loved you. I think every guy in school wanted to be with you. Even me. But you...you never so much as looked my way. Guess you thought you were too good for me."

He laughed and paused again. "Not your little sister, though. She saw me. She looked at me like I was...like I was somebody. She looked at me like nobody looked at me since..."

His voice trailed off for a moment and then hardened. "But then she left. Found herself someone new. And you, pretty girl, are going to help me bring her back. She may not love me anymore, but she does love you. She'll come to me to get you."

His voice dropped into a low growl. "And when she does come back, I'm going to make damn sure she never leaves me again."

She heard him walk away and shivered in the cool air. She had no idea what Damien was planning for Zhara, but she knew it wasn't good. There had to be a way to warn Zhara to stay away.

~ ~

Zhara was gathering up her things and preparing out the door when she heard something fall to the floor with a heavy thunk. She turned in the direction of the sound and noticed her grandpa's old rifle had fallen from its place above the door. "I'll be careful, Grandpa. I promise."

She hesitated for a moment but grabbed up the rifle and headed out the door. She tethered it to the side of her bike and gunned the engine before blowing a kiss to the front porch. "Thanks for everything, Grandpa. I'll be back soon."

She tore off down the dirt road and sped down the highway toward Mike and Gabby's place, slowing to the speed limit once she hit town. She pulled up and grabbed up her bag with the cell phone in it before running up the stairs and knocking on Mike's door. "You ready to do this?"

His eyes were filled with concern. She wanted to reassure him that everything would be okay, but it wasn't a promise she could make. If Damien was willing to go this far to get her attention, there was no telling what he was capable of doing.

She gave him a hug instead and entered the room, pulling out her cell phone and the charger from her bag. She sat on the couch and dialed Damien's number.

She wasn't conscious that she'd been holding her breath until the phone went straight to voice mail. "Damien, it's Zhara. You wanted to talk. I'm ready to talk. Just give me a call."

Her stomach clenched as she hang up the phone. She gripped it like it was a life line. It was the only thing connecting her to Gabby right then.

He put an arm around her shoulders and pulled her close. "He'll call you back. I know he will. We're going to find her. It's going to be okay."

She felt tears welling up in her eyes. "How do you know that? Everybody always says that, but nobody KNOWS that things are going to be okay. Don't make promises you can't keep, okay?"

He sighed and kissed the top of her head. "You're right. I don't know. I can't know. I'm not a fortune teller. I don't have a crystal ball. I'm just as scared and worried as you are. But I have to believe that things will be okay and that there's something greater than this moment, and a purpose that I may not understand right now but will come to see eventually. I have to believe that because the alternative is giving up and giving in, and that's not what Gabby needs me to do right now."

Tears rolled down her cheeks and she let Mike's words sink in to her soul. He was right. She had to at least believe it was possible that things would work out, otherwise the darkness she felt in her heart might just swallow her whole.

~ ~

Damien hit the button to the elevator and headed up top. There was no cell phone reception down in the bunker. The thickness of the walls and the depth of the cavern absorbed too much of the signal. It was not the way he wanted things, but it would have to do.

He stepped out of the elevator and into the morning light, squinting at the brightness of it. Sure enough, there was a missed call from Zhara.

He listened to the sound of her voice and felt a sense of smug satisfaction. He knew she'd come running back to him once she knew he had Gabby. But he wasn't ready to talk. Not yet. First, he needed a plan. A plan that would ensure that he got everything he wanted.

He wanted to be sure that Zhara understood that he was in control. This was his game and his rules. She would play by them, or Gabby would face the consequences. He was going to take this nice and slow, make her beg for mercy, make her beg to give him whatever he wanted. Once he was done, she would know who was boss.

And the first step was to get her away from everyone else. Get her alone and isolated. Then, and only then, would he talk to her.

He sent her a text message. "My house. Now. Stay until I get there.

You leave, you lose."

He thought about the possibility of her bringing Mike with her or even of her calling the cops. He added one line. "You bring friends or tell anyone where you are going, you lose."

He hit send and then headed back downstairs. He would need to take care of Gabby before leaving. This might take a while and he didn't want her to accidentally die before he had a chance to get what he needed out of her.

~ ~

Damien removed the blindfold from Gabby's eyes and uncuffed her right hand. He set an MRE and a fork in front of her before taking the gag out of her mouth. He poured a drink and set it in reach of her. "Eat up. Drink. I'm going somewhere and I won't be back for a while."

Gabby squinted as her eyes adjusted to the light. She flipped him a finger and sat back in her chair. "You might as well put the gag back in. I'm not eating this crap."

Damien shrugged and grinned at her. "Suit yourself. It's going to be a long wait till your next meal. I've got to go entertain your little sister for a while, but don't worry. I'll be back to take care of you just as soon as I'm done with her."

Gabby's eyes narrowed. "Don't you touch her, you pig. I swear to God if you hurt her, I'll kill you."

Damien laughed. "Mighty big threats coming out of your mouth right now. If I were you, Gabby, I'd be putting my mouth to much better uses. Could be if you were just nice enough to me, I wouldn't go visit Zhara at all. Maybe I'd forget all about her and stay and play some more with you."

Gabby's jaw clenched. He saw something flicker in her eyes. She tilted her head to the side and her eyes ran up his frame to meet his. "Is that the game we're playing? You promise to leave my little sister alone as long as I play nice?"

Damien crossed his arms over his chest and lifted an eyebrow. "I said maybe. Depends on how good you are at convincing me you're going to make the game worth playing. And I'm not convinced. No, not at all."

Chapter 9

"Once we step out those doors, Gabby, we are all happy, understand?" Gabby's mother squatted down so that her face was level with Gabby's. Her eyes were somber and serious.

"Because if we aren't happy, then the bad men will come and they will take you away from me again. You won't see Mike anymore. And they must not know about the bottles, okay? You can't tell them anything about those. We are happy. We love each other. And then you will be able to stay with me, and with Mike. Do you understand?"

Gabby looked down and picked at the hem of her skirt before nodding her head. She knew that her mother was right. All it would take was one word that the child services lady didn't like and they would be taken away again. Gabby had cried for months until they'd returned her to her mother and reunited her with Mike.

It wasn't her mother, so much, that she missed. She didn't miss going hungry as often as not because her mother was too drunk to cook or sleeping off a hangover. She didn't miss her mother's drunken rages. It was Mike she missed.

She would do anything to stay with him. She would lie or steal or cheat, if necessary, not to be parted from him again. It was the scariest thing that had ever happened to her and she was determined it never would again.

They stepped outside and Gabby forced all of her fear and her worry and her anger into a small corner in the back of her mind. She pushed everything she didn't want to feel away and locked it up tight inside of her.

She thought about the happiness she'd felt when Mike and she were back together again, and she let that happiness fill up all the space where the sadness and the other feelings had been.

She put on her brightest smile and held her mother's hand as she knew she must. "Hello, Gabrielle. I am glad to see you today."

Gabby smiled at the lady even though she hated being called Gabrielle. It was the name her mother called her whenever she was in trouble. "Thank you. I am glad to see you, too."

She knew how to deliver the lines she was supposed to say with conviction. Her mother had forced her to practice for hours, as if she were auditioning for a part in a play. "How have things been at home? Is Mommy cooking for you and taking care of the house?"

Gabby nodded and smiled. "Yes. Mommy cooks the best meals."

It was true. Her mother was a fabulous cook when she was sober. The problem was that she was not sober very often. "I notice you have a pretty dress on today. Did Mommy buy that for you?"

Gabby decided to treat this session like a game. She would make it her job to fool the child services lady. If the lady believed her, she got a point. If the lady didn't believe her, she lost a point.

She would see just how many points she could get before the interview was over. "My momma and I went to the mall and she let me pick this out. I love it."

It was a partial truth. The church lady came and took Gabby to the mall and picked out the dress for her. Gabby loved it.

It was her first new dress in more than a year. "Really? What store did your mommy buy that from? I have a daughter about your age and I would love to get one like it."

Gabby knew the child services lady didn't believe her all the way, not yet. Minus one point. "It was the big two-story department store. I don't remember the name, but it has an escalator inside. We rode it to the top floor to get my dress."

The client services lady nodded. "I do know that store. It's big, isn't it?"

Gabby grinned. She'd earned a point. The child services lady believed her.

Two hours later, Gabby was sitting in the waiting room, waiting for the child services lady to come out and talk to her mother. Mike was sitting beside her, holding her hand.

They both looked down the hall when they heard the lady's heels clicking on the tile floors. "I must say, Alice, your children seem to be doing very well. You've been attending your AA meetings regularly, and you have finished your parenting classes. I think we can safely restore custody of your children to you on a full-time basis. We'll have one more follow-up visit, and then everything should be all clear."

Her mother thanked the child services lady and reached for their hands. Mike took her right and she took her mother's left. They walked out into the bright sunshine and got into the car. The smile came off the moment she got in the door of her bedroom. Her face ached from it. It was exhausting playing pretend like that all the time, but if that is what it took to stay with Mike, she would do it.

~ ~

A little bit of acting and she could protect Zhara from Damien. That's all? Just a little bit of acting. She revived the game from childhood. A point if she could make him believe her. Lose a point if he doubted her. The game began now. The prize was her sister.

She gathered up all of the emotions that weren't useful to her – her fear, her anger, her worry, and even her pride and stuffed them all into her mental closet. She held his gaze while she imagined the last time she'd felt passion and desire sweep through her for a man. She held onto those feelings as she licked her lips.

She knew a lot about men. She'd grown up around the bar and men were her best friends all through childhood and into her adulthood. She knew that men were binary creatures by nature. They had exactly two heads, but – as the late Robin Williams had once stated – only blood enough to operate one at a time. All a woman needed to do to have a man under her control was to figure out which head was in operation and make sure to appeal to that one.

She tested the waters to find his baseline and unbuttoned a top button of her shirt before leaning forward. "Damien, Damien. You think I didn't notice you in high school? A man like you can't help but be noticed, but you were always busy with other girls."

She stuck out a lip as if pouting. "Maybe if you'd have let me know…"

She sighed and let her eyes trace his outline. The grin on his face widened. One point for her. "Well…and then you showed up with

Zhara. I would never, ever hurt my little sister. But that doesn't mean a girl can't be jealous, you know?"

She allowed a smile to slowly drift across her face. "Of course, now she has someone new…"

That was a mistake. She watched something shift on his face. His eyes went hard and his lips thinned into a single straight line.

He pushed away from the table and stood up. "Nice try. You really did give it your best, I'll give you that. But play time is over. Your little sister is waiting for me."

Gabby felt like cursing, but she held her cool. "Awww..and we were just getting started. You sure you don't want to stay and play? Just for a little while?"

Damien's lip curled slightly in derision. "Game's up. You might as well give it up."

She sighed and shrugged. "Could I at least go to the bathroom before you leave? I'd hate to ruin this fabulous décor here, but I'm having trouble holding it."

His eyes narrowed and he nodded his head briefly. "You get one shot at this. I'll escort you to the bathroom but if you try anything, if you try escaping, I will make sure you are tied up so tight you can't breathe, let alone move. Is that clear?"

She nodded, her eyes wide and round. She knew he meant every word. That didn't mean she wasn't going to try. She had to warn Zhara to stay away.

He grabbed hold of her right wrist and pinned it up against her back while he freed the cuff from the chair and then secured her right wrist in it. He then freed her right ankle but kept a firm grip on it before liberating the left and then locking the two back together again so that she was effectively hobbled.

He picked her up and tossed her across his shoulder, carrying her 50 feet to the bathroom and dumping her on her feet. "How am I supposed to go to the bathroom without my hands free?"

He uncuffed one hand but the chain that connected her ankle cuffs with her wrist cuffs didn't give her a lot of room to maneuver. He didn't say a word. He just turned and left her to her business.

She looked around for something, anything, that she could use to get free. There was nothing but toilet paper and a rusty sink. The floor was steel and the walls were concrete. There was no window.

Her heart sank. She was just pulling her pants up and fastening them when Damien opened the door, picked her up, and carried her back over to the chair.

He reattached her restraints, leaving her right hand free so she could eat and drink. "Don't get yourself into any trouble while I'm gone. Zhara would hate for something bad to happen to you."

Chapter 10

"Where are you going, Zhara?"

Zhara climbed onto her bike and looked at Mike. "I can't tell you. I'm sorry. Just trust me when I tell you that I have to go."

Mike crossed his arms in front of his chest and shook his head. "You're going to him, aren't you? Don't do this, Zhara. Whatever he's told you, don't do it."

Zhara started up her engine and pretended not to hear him. She was three blocks down the road, headed toward Damien's place, when she answered the question. "I'm sorry, Mike. I have to. I'd never forgive myself if something happened to Gabby because of me."

It took her 30 minutes to make her way up the steps to Damien's house. The lights were off. It was clear he wasn't home. She shuddered slightly before opening the door.

She took a step forward and heard the crunch of broken glass beneath her boot. She flipped on the lights and looked down, noticing the spray of glass shards. Her eyes followed the trail toward the place where the beer bottle hit the brick wall.

She grabbed a pan and a broom and cleaned it up more out of a desire to do something than anything else. She hated the fact that she was consigned to waiting on him, waiting for what would come next. If this was any indication of Damien's state of mind, she wasn't looking forward to their reunion.

Damien's temper had always been explosive, but the explosions were usually directed at walls or possessions. He'd never once hit her in the six years she'd known him. She'd never imagined he would do something like this, and she still couldn't understand it. This was taking things to a whole new level.

She finished cleaning up the glass and sat down on the couch with her phone in her lap. There were six text messages from Mike already. She ignored them. There was no point in replying. It wasn't going to change her mind.

There was only one person whose phone call she would answer right now: Damien's. As long as he had Gabby, she would do whatever he wanted her to do if that's what it took to keep her safe. Gabby and Mike were the sun and the moon to her.

No matter how crazy the rest of her life might get, they were the anchors that kept her grounded. They were always there for her. Now it was her turn to be there for them no matter what it cost her.

~ ~

"Damn it, Zhara." Mike swore as he watched her bike head off down the road. He hesitated for a moment and then grabbed the keys beside the door, striding toward his pickup truck. W

hatever she was doing, he wasn't going to allow her to do this on her own. He'd lost one sister to Damien, he wasn't going to lose them both.

It was his fault that Zhara even knew Damien in the first place. Damien and he were on the same football team in high school, but they'd never liked one another.

Damien was a senior when Mike was a sophomore. Damien was arrogant and brash, taking risks that put other players in harm's way. His risks often did result in touch downs and points earned, which Damien wasted no time bragging about, but at the cost of destroying other players.

Mike thought he'd seen the last of the man when Damien dropped out of high school right after football season ended, but they'd met again four years later when Mike was attending the college graduation of one of his old football buddies.

Mike brought Zhara and Gabby to the party with him. Zhara had been drawn to Damien like a fly to honey. He hadn't realized the attraction was mutual.

Six weeks later, she brought Damien to meet them. Mike took her aside and warned her about him but she wouldn't listen. She'd told him that Damien loved her and if he did anything to make Damien go away, she was going to run away and they would never hear from her again.

And he believed her. They weren't blood related. He wasn't her legal guardian. He couldn't force her to stay. So he'd kept his feelings about Damien to himself, even while he nursed her through every heartbreak and heartache the man put her through.

It seemed they broke up about every six weeks like clockwork only to come together as if they were polarized magnets that just couldn't stay apart for long. It was maddening. But there had been nothing he could do to convince her not to return to him.

Now this. If they all survived it, he hoped it would be enough to convince her to put Damien behind her for good. Maybe now she would finally listen to his warnings. He just hoped it wasn't too late.

~ ~

"Get up. Now!" Damien shook Zhara awake. Her amber eyes opened and she blinked once before standing up. She stood there, staring him in the eyes, without a word.

Always before when he'd looked at her, he'd been able to find in those eyes passion and desire, admiration, and respect. Now, all that he saw in them was fear and worry. He knew the fear and worry were there not for him, but because of him.

He felt regret and anger mingle together. "Why, Zhara? Why did you make me do this?"

Her eyes widened and her mouth opened. "I didn't make you do anything, Damien! How is this suddenly my fault?"

Rage began to fill him at her denial. "Don't you play dumb with me! YOU KNOW WHAT YOU'VE DONE! You LEFT me!"

She shook her head and her face began to turn red. "I didn't LEAVE you, Damien. You told me to GET OUT!"

His eyes narrowed and he stared at her. "You LEFT me the moment you fell in love with HIM! That's why I told you to get out!"

Tears began to fill her eyes. "What was I supposed to do, Damien? Wait around for you forever? I spent six YEARS waiting! I finally found someone who loved me and wasn't afraid to admit it."

The words lodged like an arrow in his chest. He fought against the pain that gripped his heart. Her words were confirmation of everything he feared.

He growled and grabbed her arm, leading her toward the door. "We're leaving. Now. Unless you want Gabby to keep waiting."

She tried to pull her arm away, but his grip was too tight. "Don't hurt her, Damien. If you ever loved me, if you ever even cared about me, don't hurt her. I will do whatever you want. Just don't hurt her."

He felt like shaking her until her teeth rattled in her head. Instead, he drug her over to his bike, mounted it, and looked her in the eyes. "You're damned right you'll do whatever I want. Because if you don't, Gabby will be the one to pay the price. Now get on the damn bike and shut the hell up."

He waited until he felt her arms around his waist before he gunned the motor and backed out of the driveway. He was going to make sure she never, ever left him again.

~ ~

Gabby picked at the food on her tray. She knew she should eat, but her stomach was in knots and she wasn't feeling particularly hungry. She'd failed Zhara, and now they would both pay the price.

Minutes stretched like hours as she waited for him to return. There was an awful silence in the place that deepened the feelings of loneliness and isolation that swept over her. Anxiety gripped her as she thought about what might happen if he didn't come back. Nobody would find her. Nobody would even know where to begin looking.

She laid her head on her arm and tried to block out the fear by taking a nap. It was the best way she could think of to pass the time, but no matter how hard she tried, she couldn't make herself fall asleep.

She kept thinking she heard the hum of the elevator and every time she imagined it, her heart would jump a little and she would feel a spike of excitement followed by a rush of despair when she realized it was just her imagination.

She was nearly in tears when she finally heard a voice behind her. "Look what I've brought you, Gabby. Your little sister. She's come to join our little party."

She jumped and turned her head. It was true. Damien led Zhara to the table and pulled up a chair for her. She felt guilty at how happy the sight of the two of them made her feel.

"Sit." He gave the command to Zhara and she sat without a word. Her eyes connected briefly with Gabby's before she looked back down at the table.

Gabby frowned as she watched the exchange. "She's not a dog, you know."

Damien grinned. "Oh, but she is. She's my bitch now. Aren't you, Zhara?"

Zhara didn't look up. "Yes, sir."

Gabby's eyes narrowed. "You bastard."

Damien grabbed a handful of Zhara's hair and forced her head backward. He kissed her while his eyes were locked on Gabby's and then let her go. Gabby could see tears in Zhara's eyes, but she didn't complain or resist.

"I seem to recall you singing a different tune before Zhara got here. I may be a bastard, but I'm the bastard in charge, and the two of you are under my command. Isn't that right, Zhara?"

Zhara looked down at the table. "Yes, sir."

Gabby felt sick at her stomach. There had to be a way out of this. She would find it or die trying. There was no way she was going to leave her little sister in the hands of this man.

Chapter 11

"Daddy's dead, Mike. You have to be the man of the house now. No more crying. You have to take care of Gabby and me, understand?"

Mike wiped the tears from his eyes and nodded at his mother. She ruffled his dark curls briefly and wiped her own tears away. She reached for his hand and he took it.

"Come on. We have to go back inside." Mike stood up and followed her inside where the rest of the funeral guests were gathered.

He straightened his shoulders and walked over to where Gabby was seated. She turned toward him and buried her face in his shoulder, sobbing. He didn't say anything. He just held her and let her cry. He felt his own tears welling up inside him but shoved them back down. He had to be a man now, and men didn't cry.

His grandfather came over and sat down beside them without a word. He patted Mike's shoulder. "It's going to be okay."

Mike didn't know what to say to that, so he didn't say anything. He didn't know how anything would ever be okay again.

"You're going to be okay. I promise you that. You and your sister and your mother. I'll make sure you don't lack for anything."

Mike frowned. There was nothing that would bring his father back to life again. They would always lack for that.

"I should have been there for him. I didn't know. He never told me. I'm sorry."

Those were words that Mike heard out of so many mouths at that funeral home that day, along with one big word: "suicide" that was spoken in low tones by some of them when they thought Mike couldn't hear it. Later, when they got home that night, Mike sought his mother out. "What does soo-ee-side mean, Momma?"

His mother's grey eyes darkened for a moment as she looked at him. Her mouth opened briefly and then shut, as if she wanted to tell him something but didn't know how. She sighed and sat down at the kitchen table. "Suicide means that someone took their own life. They chose to die."

Mike's eyes widened. He didn't want this to be true. "Did Daddy do that? Did he choose to die?"

His mother's shoulders slumped and she looked away. Mike didn't need to hear her say it. He knew the answer.

"But why? Why, Momma? Why did he choose to die? Didn't he love us?"

A tear streaked down her face followed by another. Mike regretted asking, but he needed to hear the answer. Her voice cracked when she spoke finally. "Baby, sometimes love just isn't enough. Sometimes the darkness inside us is so deep that the love can't reach us. I think that's how it was with your daddy. He loved us, but it just wasn't enough to break through the darkness inside him. The darkness swallowed him up."

Mike frowned, pondering her words. How could he be sure it wouldn't happen to him? "How come he got swallowed up by the darkness?"

His mother sighed and looked at him. She kissed his forehead. "I don't know, Baby. I don't know. I did everything I could, but it wasn't enough. It just wasn't enough."

~ ~

Mike cursed as he lost sight of Zhara for a moment and then breathed a sigh of relief as he caught sight of the bike again. He saw her pull up to the front of a single-story Craftsman style home in a run-down part of town. Damien's house. She hesitated for a moment before opening the door and walking inside.

What she was doing there? He spent hours watching the house, bored out of his mind. It was after ten o'clock when a motorcycle with a familiar figure pulled up into the driveway. Damien. Thirty minutes later, he watched Damien dragging Zhara out of the house. She didn't look happy to see him.

He was too far away to hear their conversation, but her eyes widened and her face paled. She climbed on back of his bike and the two of them took off. He waited until they were a block ahead of him before following them.

Mike grew concerned when the route they were taking led to an old military base on the edge of town. He'd been here once on a school field trip, but not since it closed down. Damien pulled off the road and followed a trail that led into the base.

Mike didn't dare follow after him this time. If he had Gabby, who knew what he might do if he felt threatened. For her sake, he couldn't afford to be spotted.

He sped past the place and waited until he was a safe distance away before pulling a u-turn and heading back to town. Now that he at least knew where Damien was holing up, it was time to get some supplies. He gunned the truck, heading straight for Purgatory.

He'd promised his mother that he would take care of Gabby, and he wasn't about to break that promise now. "I'm coming for you, Gabby. Just hold tight."

It took him 45 minutes to make his way back to town and 20 minutes more to pull into the parking lot of Purgatory. He unlocked the door and walked inside. He was almost finished gathering up the things he thought he might need when he heard a loud rapping on the front door of the bar. Annoyed, he went up front to tell whomever it was that they were closed.

He pulled open the door and was surprised to find John standing there. "What are you doing here?"

John looked at the rucksack that Mike was toting. "I was looking for Zhara. Is she here?"

Mike shifted. "No. I'm on my way to get her."

John nodded. "Might I come with you? I really need to speak with her."

Mike shook his head. "I don't think it's a good idea. Things are likely to get rough and I can't afford to protect anybody else. I'll have my hands full trying to deal with Damien and keep both Gabby and Zhara safe."

Something flickered in John's eyes. John's speech was careful and clipped. "What do you mean deal with Damien? What's happened?"

Mike hesitated. He knew the man cared about Zhara, but time was wasting and he needed to get out there. Something told him to trust John. "Damien's kidnapped my sister. The police won't do anything about it for at least 72 hours, but I don't know if she's got that long. Truth is, I don't know what he's capable of doing."

John's eyebrows raised. "And Zhara?"

Mike winced. "She went to try and get Damien to let Gabby go, but now he's got them both. Look, I don't have a lot of time to stand here explaining things. I can't stop you from following me if you're determined, but I can't guarantee you aren't going to get hurt. Just make sure you don't get in my way."

John pulled himself up to his full height and stood looking at Mike. "You needn't worry about me. I can take care of myself. But if there's a chance that Zhara needs me, I'm not going to stand by and do nothing."

Mike nodded and opened the door to let the man in. "Help yourself to whatever's behind the bar. I'm going to head to the office to make a few phone calls before we leave."

John lifted an eyebrow. "I would hardly think that this is a time for drinking. I doubt liquid courage is going to give us an edge in rescuing the ladies."

Mike grinned. "Liquor bottles make for surprisingly effective weapons if you have a lighter and an igniter. All you need to do is stick something like a wick inside the bottle, ignite the wick, and toss the bottle inside. Instant Molotov cocktail. There's some bar rags behind there. Grab a few of those. We can use them for wicks. Be sure to grab some lighters, too."

John stared at Mike as if he couldn't believe what he was hearing. "Don't you think that's a little…extreme? Aren't we likely to get the ladies hurt along with Damien?"

Mike shrugged and continued walking toward the office. "If you knew Damien like I do, you'd know that Damien's like a bull dog. He's not going to let go of what he's gotten hold of without somebody forcing his jaws apart. I don't want to need to use these, but I also want to be prepared for whatever we might be facing."

He left John behind and opened the door to the office. He grabbed up the cash box and picked up the phone. "Edward? I know it's late, man, but I have a favor to ask of you."

Thirty minutes later, he and John headed out the door on their way to the military base.

~ ~

"What do you want from us, Damien?" Gabby glared at Damien, her green eyes like twin emeralds in the pale ivory of her face.

Damien leaned back in his seat and pulled out a fifth of whiskey, setting it in the center of the table. He pulled out three shot glasses and set one in front of each person. "The truth I want the truth."

Gabby's eyes narrowed as she glanced at the bottle and back at his face. "What's your game?"

Damien shrugged, opened the bottle, and poured a generous measure into each shot glass. "It's a guessing game. We take turns guessing things about each other. If the person guessing something is right, you drink. If they're wrong, you don't have to drink. It's an easy enough game."

Zhara didn't look at her shot glass. She just continued staring at the table. Damien grabbed a handful of hair and yanked her head closer to his so that she was forced to look him in the eyes. "Better play nice, Zhara, or I'll have to put you in the corner and play with Gabby all by myself."

Zhara's teeth clenched and her jaw tightened. "Let me go! I'll do whatever you want. I'll play your stupid game. Just leave Gabby alone."

Damien loosened his grip, but didn't let go. "That's a good girl. Now apologize."

Zhara closed her eyes and swallowed. Her voice was controlled and low. Damien recognized it as Zhara at her most dangerous. "I'm sorry. Let go, PLEASE."

Damien let go of her hair but grabbed her wrist and snaked an arm around her waist. "Give me a kiss. Show me you mean it."

She closed her eyes and kissed him, but it lacked any fire or passion at all. It was as cold a kiss as he'd ever been given by her. He frowned and pulled his arm away from her waist. She sat back down without a word. "First guess is for you, Gabby. I'm going to guess that you're still a virgin."

Gabby lifted an eyebrow and matched his stare without flinching. He was surprised when she took a drink and slammed the shot glass on the table. He tabled his fingers beneath his chin, grinned at her, and poured another drink in her shot glass. She ignored him and turned to Zhara.

"My turn. My guess is for Zhara. I'm going to guess that you didn't tell Mike where you were going." Zhara drank her shot. Damien's eyes narrowed as he watched them but he didn't say anything. He just reached for the bottle of whiskey and refilled her shot glass. Zhara turned toward him.

Her face was impassive but her eyes were devoid of their usual warmth. "My guess is for Damien. I'm going to guess that you've never loved anybody but yourself."

He felt red creeping up his face but he kept his eyes fastened on hers and he didn't take a drink. She returned his stare for a moment before they both looked away. She crossed her arms in front of her chest.

"My guess is for Gabby. I'm going to guess that you know the name of the man that Zhara is currently dating."

Gabby rolled her eyes but didn't take a drink. Damien looked over at Zhara. She shrugged and he smirked at Gabby. Gabby locked eyes with Damien. "My guess is for you, Damien. I'm going to guess that you don't have a good relationship with your mom."

Damien felt as if her words had struck him physically. He held her eyes, picked up his shot and drank it without a word, slamming the glass against the steel table with enough force to put a crack in it. He reached across the table for the bottle of whiskey and poured himself another shot. "Drink up, ladies. We're done with this game."

Damien drank down his shot and waited for the ladies to finish theirs. Neither of them moved. It was like they were ignoring him. He stood up and slammed his hands on the table, making both of them jump. "I *said* drink up. You drink up, or you'll get to watch as your sister pays the price."

Zhara and Gabby looked at one another. They both drank their shots. Damien smirked. "You're learning. That's good. Now, Zhara, it's time for you to go to bed. Gabby and I have some talking to do."

He grabbed Zhara's arm and led her to a back room. Gabby struggled against the bonds that held her to the chair. Her face went red. "You leave her alone! You bastard!"

Gabby's screams echoed in his ears as he shoved Zhara onto the bed and shut the heavy metal door behind them, blocking out the sound.

Chapter 12

"Come on, come on!" Mike pushed the limits of his pickup's speedometer to its maximum, zipping in and out of traffic on his way back to the base.

John was firmly gripping the bar above the passenger side door. "Do you always drive like this?"

Mike grimaced as he nearly collided with a car in front of him and managed to swerve into the next lane at the last minute. "Only when my sisters are in the hands of a maniac."

John closed his eyes for a moment as Mike floored it through a red light at an intersection. "You do realize it won't help them if we don't make it there alive?"

Mike gritted his teeth, suddenly regretting his decision to let John come with him. "You know what really won't help? You distracting me. Now, make a choice: shut up or get the hell out. Pick one."

John took a deep breath as if he were about to say something and then clenched his jaw. It was obvious that he wasn't backing out of this. Mike returned his eyes to the road.

"Glad we have an understanding. Let's go get our girls."

~ ~

"What are you doing with my clothes?" Zhara stared at Damien. There was a red spot on her cheek from where he'd slapped her once and bite marks all along her neck. He'd never exactly been tender with her in bed, but he'd never hurt her this badly before. It was as if he'd taken every bit of anger he felt and poured it into her.

Damien paused for a moment after gathering them up and looked at her, his eyes glittering dangerously. "I'm getting rid of them. You don't need them. When I want you dressed, I'll dress you."

Zhara stood up to stop him and he backhanded her. She stumbled back against the bed railing and sat back down, hard. "If I want you up off that bed, I'll get you up off it myself. You'll stay there and you'll wait for me."

He sneered at her. "I've got business with your sister. Try to get some sleep. This may take a while."

Zhara glared at him. "What are you going to do to her?"

He laughed. It was low and dark and ugly. "The same thing I do to you. Whatever the hell I want."

He yanked open the door and walked out, slamming the thick metal door behind him. She tried the doorknob, but it was locked tight.

Zhara beat on the door. "Let me out! Damien, please! Let me out!"

There was no response. She sat back down on the bed, blinking back tears. She had no way of knowing what he was doing to Gabby and no way of helping her even if she did know. She couldn't even help herself. "I don't know what to do, Grandpa. I don't know what to do."

She tucked her legs up against her chest and wrapped her arms around them. She hadn't felt this hopeless and this helpless in a very long time, not since the day she found her Grandpa dead beneath that tree. She buried her face in her knees and began to cry tears of rage and frustration as she rocked herself back and forth.

She cried until she didn't have a single tear left in her and lay back on the bed wishing she were dead. She blamed herself for all of it. If not for her, Gabby wouldn't be in there with Damien. If not for her, Gabby and Mike would never have been dragged into all of this.

The weight of guilt and the shame she carried for what she'd allowed him to do to her were like anchors weighing down her soul. She couldn't protect the people she loved no matter how hard she tried. She couldn't stop them from leaving her. She lay there and closed her eyes, drifting off to sleep.

"I'll never let anything happen to you, Zhara girl. That's a promise."

The voice was so clear and so close at hand that it startled her awake. The strong scent of wood smoke and fresh turned earth surrounded her as if it were a shield protecting her.

It was so distinctive, so clear to her, that she knew she wasn't just imagining it. She felt like if she just reached out her hand, she could touch her grandfather. However, there was nothing in front of her but empty space.

Zhara felt hope flicker to life. Her eyes told her that she was alone, but her heart disagreed, and she trusted her heart. Somehow, she was going to get out of this, and Gabby was going to get out of it with her.

~ ~

Gabby heard Zhara cry out once before the door was shut and then there was silence. After what seemed to her like forever, Damien exited the room, zipping up his pants as he strode toward her. "What did you do to her?"

Damien grinned. "Nothing she didn't want done. Your little sister likes it rough. Or didn't you know that."

Gabby frowned. "I swear to you if you've hurt her."

Damien crossed his arms over his chest. "Yeah? You've already threatened me. Do I look scared to you?"

Gabby sat back but kept her eyes on him. "What do you want with me, Damien?"

He reached out and picked up a strand of her hair and stretched it taut before letting it go. "What do you think I want with you?"

Gabby stared at him. "If you wanted that, you could have taken it before now. Why wait? Why wait until Zhara's here? Does it make you happy to hurt her like that? Is that how you get your thrills?"

He laughed and leaned forward. "Don't you worry about little Zhara. She's locked inside that room. What she doesn't know won't hurt her. Why now? Before now, I didn't know you were a virgin. Now I do. But you won't be after tonight."

Gabby felt a cold chill run down her spine, but she kept her face straight and her voice low. "You don't want to do that."

Damien walked behind her, grabbed her right hand, and cuffed it to the back of her chair. Then he reached over and unbuttoned the top button of her shirt.

"No? And why don't I want to do that? Because it would hurt poor little Zhara's feelings? Bitch didn't care about mine when she found her new boyfriend. Seems to me like screwing you is the perfect revenge on the both of you. You always looked at me like I was nothing. You won't be looking at me like that once I'm through with you."

Gabby's mind raced for a reason that might stop him. She forced a laughed. "No, you jackass. You think raping me is going to make me respect you? You have got to be the dumbest man I have ever met. I'm telling you that you don't want to do this because you don't want to catch what I've got. There's a reason I'm still a virgin, and it isn't because I don't like men."

Damien jerked the cloth of her blouse so hard it popped the second button off. His voice was a low growl. He was angry. "You think I'm stupid, bitch? Tell me you're a virgin and then tell me you have an STD? I don't buy it. I think you just want to spoil my fun. I'm going to make our time together extra,"

He bit the side of her neck and she yelped. "special. I'm going to really enjoy that tight ass of yours."

She dug the nails of her fingers into her palm as he plunged his hand down into her bra, fighting for control over her emotions. She hoped he couldn't hear the fear in her voice. "Your funeral, asshole. I got my STD from a blood transfusion when I was a kid. If you weren't so stupid you'd know you don't have to have sex to get those. Kissing, sex, blood transfusions...any of those can do it. Or did you skip health class the way you skipped everything else?"

He pinched her nipple hard enough it brought tears to her eyes. "That may be true but that doesn't mean I can't still have a good time. It just means I'll have to be more creative about how I enjoy myself."

Gabby swallowed back tears as he took his hand away long enough to undo the third button. Her chest was now completely exposed and the black bra beneath on full display.

She struggled to control her breathing. She didn't want him to know how scared she was. Fear was like food for bullies. She decided to try a bit of distraction. "Tell me about your mom."

His hand froze on its way to the fourth button. As she'd noticed earlier, his mother was a weak point in his armor. It wasn't much, but it was all she had going for her.

His voice was a low growl in her ear. "There's nothing to tell. The bitch left when I was just 8 years old. I haven't seen her since."

Gabby frowned and closed her eyes as his hands tugged her shirt front out of her waist band. She was starting to feel woozy. Despite tending bar for years, she'd never been much of a drinker.

To make matters worse, she hadn't had anything but the MRE to eat in the last 36 hours. The alcohol was hitting her harder and faster than it might have otherwise.

Damien seemed to notice it. He reached across her and poured another shot of whiskey into her glass, then brought it up to her lips. "Drink it."

She shook her head and tried to clamp her lips shut. He pinched her nose shut, forcing her to open her mouth to breathe and poured the whiskey down her throat. She choked on it as it went down the wrong way and coughed to clear her airways. She shook her head. "No. No more."

He ignored her and poured another. "Drink it."

She shook her head, but he grabbed a handful of her hair and held her head in place.

"I said DRINK IT!"

Tears slid down her face as she drank the shot. She watched him pour another. She knew all about alcohol poisoning.

She was about six shots away from death's door according to her calculations, and that was only if her body could metabolize it at a normal rate. She wasn't sure it could. "Damien, please no. Please don't. No more."

He pushed the table back a ways and pulled his chair up in front of hers. She was struggling to focus. He took the shot and drank it. "Don't worry. This one's for me, not for you. Can't let you have fun all by yourself."

The last thing she remembered before passing out was the flash of a camera.

Chapter 13

"I'm not afraid of you ANYMORE!" Zhara stood her ground, glaring at the boy, daring him to try and get up. Her fist was raised and ready to strike.

"That's enough out of you, young lady."

Zhara's eyes didn't leave the boy's, but she lowered her fist.

"We don't hit people." Her foster mother came into the room and put out a hand to the boy, who accepted her help while smirking at Zhara.

"She hit me again, Mom! I wasn't even doing anything to her."

Zhara's face flushed red. "He's LYING, Mrs. Morris. He was…"

Mrs. Morris frowned at Zhara before holding up a hand and cutting her off. "We've talked about this before, Zhara. I don't care what Sean did. You can't keep hitting people. I understand that you're having trouble adjusting, but hitting people is not an appropriate way to express yourself. Go to your room."

Zhara glared at Sean and crossed her arms over her chest as she left the room headed for the bedroom they'd given her. She shut the door behind her and flopped onto the bed. There had to be a way to stop Sean. There had to be.

Sean was 13 years old, but already a match for his father in height. He towered over Zhara's petite frame. When she'd first arrived, he'd acted so nice. He would go out of his way to bring her things or do things for her.

But then he'd started demanding that she do things for him. Things that made her feel sick to her stomach and dirty. When she wouldn't do them, he'd pin her down and make her. She was afraid of him.

He told her if she told anyone else what he was doing to her, his parents would call child services and have her taken away. For nine months, she endured it and hoped he would stop. But he never did. He just kept doing more and more.

She started fighting back. Now, he would run to his mother and tell her that Zhara was being mean to him. His mother never asked any questions. She always believed everything that Sean told her. Zhara felt trapped, helpless, and angry at the same time.

Hitting him hadn't worked. Letting him have his way hadn't worked. He'd just done more and more to her. Trying to speak up for herself hadn't worked. What did she have to do to protect and defend herself? She didn't really want to hurt him. She just wanted to make him stop.

She frowned. There was only one way she knew of to make sure this stopped for good. She was going to run away. She grabbed her school backpack and stuffed it full of clothes. She didn't have any money, but she didn't care. She would go as fast as she could as far as she could so that Sean could never touch her again.

She finished packing the backpack, opened the window, and climbed out. That was the last she ever saw of the Morris family.

~ ~

Damien pulled out his cell phone and snapped the first picture right as Gabby's eyes were rolling into her head. Her head fell backward, her body went limp, and her red gold hair streamed out behind her like a banner. He was pretty sure it wasn't an act, but he needed to be 100% sure before he made his next move.

He whistled to himself as he opened up her blouse even more and took a few more shots with her bra on. She didn't move. Her breathing remained nice and even. He took out his pocket knife and slipped it through the lace of her bra and waited to see if she would respond. She didn't.

He sliced cleanly through the fabric, exposing her breasts fully, before taking a few more pictures and then walked around behind her, unlocking the cuffs that held her chained to the chair. With as much liquor as Gabby had consumed, Damien didn't expect her to wake for some time.

He spent the next hour posing her in different positions while taking pictures. He was careful to keep himself out of the frames. He didn't want any proof that he was the source of them. These would give him all the leverage he needed to ensure her silence. One word out of her mouth and he would be sure she became the newest internet porn star.

He'd wanted to take Gabby's virginity as a final coup de gras, but he wasn't sure that she wasn't telling the truth about having some disease and he didn't want to risk it. With these, he could always use them to blackmail her into sleeping with him if he found out she'd been lying.

The pictures would also serve to keep Zhara firmly under his control. If she left him or threatened to leave him again, all he had to do was threaten to post the pictures on the internet and she'd do whatever he wanted. She was so protective of Gabby.

Damien hated how closely knit they were. It always made him feel like an outsider, like he didn't really belong. He envied the sense of family that Mike and Gabby and Zhara shared even as he despised how weak it made them. Their love for each other made it all too easy to manipulate them.

That was one thing his father had gotten right. "Love makes you weak, boy. And weak people get eaten by this world."

He finished taking pictures and yawned. He was getting pretty tired. He doubted he would sleep longer than Gabby, but he didn't want to risk it, either. He couldn't afford for her to escape before she knew about the pictures. He also didn't want to chance her choking on her own vomit and dying. She would need to be watched.

He laid Gabby down on the floor just outside the door where he was keeping Zhara and grabbed the keys out of his pants pocket. He unlocked the door and pulled it open, picked up Gabby, and dumped her body on the bed next to Zhara. "Keep an eye on your sister. She wore herself out playing with me and drank too much. You want to make sure she doesn't choke on her own vomit and die."

Zhara looked from her sister back to him. He turned toward the door and pulled it open. She frowned as she watched him, but she didn't make a move to stop him. "Where are you going?"

He reached out a hand and caressed her cheek where a bruise was starting to form. She flinched but didn't pull away. "Me? I'm going home to get some sleep. Don't you worry, though. We'll have plenty of time to play together again once I've had some rest."

~ ~

Damien turned to head toward the door and Zhara knew this was her only chance to escape. If he shut that door and locked them in, they had no chance whatsoever. The door was thick steel designed to be impenetrable. She'd worn herself out trying to open it the first time he'd locked her in there. She wasn't going to allow him to lock her in there twice.

She stood up and wrapped her arms around Damien, pressing her naked breasts against him. "Are you sure you want to leave?"

Her hands travelled down his chest and she kissed his spine. She needed to keep him distracted long enough that she could grab the keys out of his pants pocket. Her voice was sultry and low. "We could have so much fun together."

Damien turned to face her and he pulled her closer to him. "That's my Zhara. I knew you'd come back around. All you needed was a little persuading."

She let her hands travel even lower, tugging on the waistband of his jeans as if she were impatient for him as he kissed her. A few more inches and she could get a hand into his pocket and fish that key out. Once she had it, it didn't matter what else happened.

She pouted as she leaned against him, deliberately slurring her words as if the alcohol were affecting her. "Come on, Damien. Don't make me beg for it. You know I want you."

She reached for the button of his pants and began unfastening it as he kissed the nape of her neck.

"You want it, baby?"

She made the appropriate noises while she slid the zipper down and started working his pants down his hips, sliding a hand into the pocket where the key was kept.

"Oh, yes. You know I want it."

He grinned and grabbed her hand. "Why don't you get on your knees and show me how much you want it?"

She kissed a trail down his chest headed toward his navel and got on her knees, pulling his pants the rest of the way down as she went. She was grateful that Gabby wasn't awake to witness any of this.

For now, all that mattered was making sure Damien didn't wise up to her real purpose until it was too late for him to stop her. With his pants off, it would be much easier to get the key out without him noticing.

He rested up against the door jam and put his hands on her head, holding her in place. She managed to slide the key out of the pocket while his eyes were closed and tucked it under her knee.

He finished and grinned down at her. "Too bad for you. Guess you'll have to wait until tomorrow to get what you want."

She pouted and made an effort to protest. "No, Damien. Don't go."

He shoved her roughly away from him. "That's enough fun for tonight. I'll come back tomorrow when your sister's awake. Maybe we'll all three of us have fun."

He slid his pants back on while she stayed where she was, not daring to move lest he spot the key. She waited until the door was shut and Damien's footsteps faded away before she dared to get back up. It was time to get out of here while the getting was good.

Chapter 14

Damien sped past a pair of headlights pointed in the direction of the military base on his way back home. There were some small farms surrounding the base that also used this road, but he doubted most of the farmers would be out this late. Instinct told him to follow that vehicle.

He cut off his headlights and flipped a u-turn, following the truck through the darkness as it turned off at the military base. He was too far away to clearly see the license plate, but he watched as two figures descended from the truck. One of them grabbed something from the back of the truck and made short work of the lock that kept the base protected from those who weren't intended to be there.

He heard Mike's voice and the voice of Zhara's new boyfriend carried to him on the wind and cursed. He pulled his bike back over to the road. He watched as they drove the truck through the gates. It might take them a while to find the bunker, especially in the dark, but it was inevitable that they would. He turned his headlights back on, and sped toward his own place. It was time to get out of town for a while.

He gathered up some of his clothes and tossed them into a duffle bag. He was glad he'd thought to get those photos of Gabby. Once the girls realized what he could do to her, they would refuse to co-operate with the police. Without the girls to testify against him, the police wouldn't be able to do anything about the situation. All he had to do was lay low for a little while and this whole thing would blow over.

He sent a text message to Zhara's phone. "There's plenty more where this one came from. Betray me and I'll make her famous. Play time's not over yet."

He selected one of his favorite photos of Gabby and sent it to her. He knew that one would get the message across. Thirty minutes later, he was ready to go.

He thought about going back to the base just to be sure the girls were safe. He was the only one who knew their exact location. It could take days or even weeks for someone else to find them. His conscience sputtered to life for a moment. As quickly as it spoke, though, he killed it with a shrug. Let Zhara's new boyfriend and Mike be responsible for them.

He drove for two hours straight before he felt safe enough to pull over at a roadside inn. It took a while to get the night clerk's attention, but he was in bed before dawn with the curtains drawn tight. Gabby and Zhara may have gotten away from him for now, but he would be back to claim them both. This wasn't over by a long shot. Not until he was ready for it to be over.

~ ~

Mike cut through the bolts securing the base and got back in the truck. They were fifty feet inside when the road became impassable. Mike grabbed a flashlight out of the back and tossed a second one to John. They both grabbed a bag of supplies.

"Looks like we're on foot from here out. Be ready for anything."

They explored the area. There were several old buildings on base. Dirt and debris filled the floors. It was clear no one had been in these for some time.

They made their way to an open field with a massive concrete dome in the center. The two men looked at one another and nodded. If there was a place where Damien was keeping the girls, it was a safe bet this was it. The question was how to get inside.

They made a loop around, looking for the entrance doors and found a pair of metal doors. A panel with a large button stood to its right.

Mike tested the doors. "They aren't moving."

John reached over and pushed the button. The sound of gears turning and metal clanking interrupted the otherwise quiet night. The doors slid open to reveal a freight elevator. Mike stepped onto it and waited for John to follow.

Judging by the control panel on the elevator, there were four full floors worth of building to search. Mike tried to control his anxiety. Gabby had already been missing more than 24 hours. Zhara had been gone a full 12. God alone knew how long it would take him to find them and what he would find once he did.

He tensed. Every second counted. Every moment was one more moment that Gabby and Zhara were in danger. He didn't know where to start or where to begin to find them. John reached over and pushed the 4th button.

"We will find them, Mike. We will begin at the lowest level and work our way up to the top. But we will find them."

Mike found himself both grateful for John's presence and irritated by it at the same time. "How can you stay so calm?"

John looked over at Mike. "Because Zhara needs me to be calm. The last thing she needs right now is for me to fall to pieces, even though that's exactly what I feel like doing. Am I frightened for her? Most definitely. Do I worry that something will happen to her beyond what already has? Of course. But none of that will help her. So I push it to the back of my mind and I focus on what I have to do right now to get closer to her. And right now, that means staying calm, thinking things through, and taking what action I can. It means trusting that good will come of even this."

Mike snorted at that last bit. "I don't see how anything good can come of this."

John looked up at the ceiling and leaned against the elevator wall. "Neither do I, at this exact moment, but that's the benefit of faith. I do not have to see it in order to believe it. I rely on years and years of accumulated data to support my conclusion, much as you and I are relying upon the laws of physics to carry us safely down to the 4th floor although we cannot see those laws. We know them and we trust them to work for us based on the fact that they always have before this point."

~ ~

Zhara waited until she was certain that Damien was gone before she opened up the door. Dragging Gabby out of the bed was harder than she'd thought it would be. She was 125 pounds of dead weight. Zhara was only 110 pounds. She frowned and thought through the best plan of attack, the one that allowed her to move at the fastest pace while doing the least amount of damage to either Gabby or herself.

She walked back out into the center room. A single light illuminated the area where the table was. Gabby's pants and underwear were piled up on top of that, along with the clothing that Damien had taken from her. She shivered slightly in the cool air as she put her clothes back on and grabbed up Gabby's pants.

It took her a little time to wrestle Gabby's inert body back into the pants, but eventually they were both at least mostly dressed. It was time to go looking for something that might help her carry Gabby's weight out of there. She needed a blanket or something like it to roll Gabby onto so she could slide her down the concrete floors.

That's when she heard the familiar hum of the elevator. Had Damien realized that he'd left the key behind and returned? She swore under her breath and looked for something, anything, that she could use as a weapon. She was not going to let herself and Gabby be retaken by that bastard if there was anything at all that she could do about it.

She grabbed the empty bottle of whiskey from the center of the table and made her way back to the room where Gabby was as quietly as possible, shutting the door most of the way behind her but leaving it open just a crack so that she could hear what was happening.

The elevator stopped and she heard two pairs of footsteps echoing in the room. Two pairs? Familiar voices drifted to her ears, voices she was all too happy to hear. Her heart raced.

Irrational fears that this was all some elaborate trick Damien concocted to get her to reveal herself flitted through her brain. She ignored her fears and opened the door. "Mike? John? In here!"

The two men turned toward the sound of her voice and hurried over. "Thank God you're okay! Where's Damien?"

She shook her head. "I don't know. He left. He said he was going to get some sleep. I guess he was headed back toward his house."

Mike looked at Zhara, an unspoken question in his eyes.

"Gabby's sleeping. I don't know what he did to her. We were apart for a little while."

Mike's brows drew together and Zhara opened the door so he could get to her. He went in and knelt beside Gabby, picking her up in his arms. John hugged Zhara. "Let's go. I think you've been here long enough, don't you?"

Zhara melted into his embrace, allowing herself to relax. It was hard to believe this was finally over. Everything was over.

Chapter 15

Gabby's head was pounding. She felt like her skull was going to crack open at any moment. She tensed up, wondering where Damien was and where he'd taken her. She expected to feel restraints but her hands and legs were free. The bed beneath her was soft and she dared to crack open an eye and look around.

Bright fluorescent lights shone overhead. White walls and tile ceilings told her she wasn't in the bunker anymore. She looked over and noticed Mike sound asleep in the chair beside her bed. She relaxed as she took in her surroundings. She was in a hospital.

Mike opened his eyes and looked at her with a smile. "Hey. You're awake. Took you long enough to join us."

Gabby tried to crack a smile but winced as another wave of pain washed over her. "Where am I? What's happening?"

Mike frowned briefly and then took her hand. "We brought you to the hospital so doctors could look you over. Zhara wasn't sure exactly what Damien might have done to you. The results from the rape kit should be back shortly."

Gabby wanted to throw up. The thought of doctors probing her and examining her without her knowledge or consent made her uneasy. "He didn't rape me, Mike. He was afraid to."

Mike lifted an eyebrow. "Why's that?"

Gabby laughed, but the sound was lacking in any humor. "I lied and told him I had a sexually transmitted disease. I told him that's why I was still a virgin."

Mike's eyes widened and he grinned. "You always were the smart one. Good thinking on your part. Still, we didn't know that and I wanted to be sure that none of the evidence had a chance to be washed away."

Gabby frowned, but didn't say anything. She knew Mike was just trying to help. "When can I go home? I just want to forget about all of this. I want to get into my own clothes and sleep in my own bed."

Mike looked at his watch. "I'll go let the nurses know you're awake. We should be able to check out in about 15 minutes."

Gabby sat up and waited for her head to stop spinning before she put her feet on the floor. "Where are my clothes? I want to get dressed."

Mike pointed to a pile of clothing. "Fortunately, the only thing he destroyed seems to have been your bra."

Gabby glanced up at Mike. "My bra?"

He nodded and looked at his hands. "That's part of the reason we felt running the rape kit was in order. I don't know what he might have done while you were passed out."

Gabby shivered despite the warmth of the room. She waited until

Mike left and closed the door behind him to get dressed. She tried to hold it together but felt tears running down her cheeks. Damn Damien to hell. The man might not have physically violated her, but God alone knew what else he'd done to her.

She pulled a trash can over and heaved into it. There was nothing in her stomach but bile. She collapsed beside the trash can and began to sob. Every ounce of fear and helplessness and rage came out of her in those tears.

Mike opened the door and gathered her into his arms. "It's okay, Gabby. It's going to be okay."

Those words just made her angry. "It's NOT okay. Nothing is okay. Nothing is ever going to be okay again!"

He stopped talking and just held onto her.

"I hate him. I hate his face. I hate everything about him." She sobbed into his shoulder until there she couldn't feel anything anymore. Mike didn't say a word. He just kept holding her, waiting for her to finish.

"Come on. Let's get you out of here and back home."

~ ~

Zhara's phone beeped softly. She picked it up off the table, hoping to hear from Mike or Gabby that everything was okay at the hospital. To her surprise, she found two text messages from Damien. Her stomach clenched. What could he possibly have to say to her?

She read the first one. "There's plenty more where this one came from. Betray me and I'll make her famous. Play time's not over yet."

She hesitated before opening the second one. It was a picture of Gabby, naked, legs spread wide, breasts on full display, face clearly visible. "Oh, God."

Her stomach sank. She finally had the answer to what he'd been doing with Gabby in the time they'd spent apart down in the bunker. The realization hit her. Damien was never going to let her go.

No matter how far she ran, no matter how hard she fought, he would always find a way to drag her back into his madness. She was going to be bound to him for as long as they both lived. He was going to make sure of it.

There was only one way to end this. There was only one way to make sure that the people she loved were protected from him. Damien had to die. She was the only one who could make it happen, the only one he would allow close enough to him to make it possible.

She sent him a text message in reply. One that she was sure he would both believe and not be able to resist at the same time. "I'm sorry. Please forgive me. This is all my fault. I'll do whatever you want. Just don't hurt Gabby. Tell me where to meet you. I'll come alone. I won't tell anyone."

She didn't have long to wait for his reply. He sent her an address and a time, nothing more. The meeting was hours away.

She took her time getting ready, selecting an outfit that she knew Damien preferred and putting on his favorite perfume. The smell of it disgusted her but this wasn't about what she wanted anymore. This was about making sure that Damien never again had the power to hurt anyone she loved.

She looked at herself in the mirror and steeled herself for what she was about to do. Killing Damien would change everything. There was no coming back from this, but she didn't see that she had a choice. It was either allow Damien to continue destroying her life and the lives of those she loved, or destroy him so that he couldn't touch anyone anymore.

She wondered what her grandfather would say if he knew what she was planning to do. She didn't allow herself to think about what John might say if he knew.

John belonged to an entirely different world than she did. His was a world of civil language and conversations. He would never understand, but this was as much for him as it was for everyone else.

If she got caught, she would go to jail. It's possible she would even be given the death penalty. Still, it was better that she should suffer than that she should make everyone else around her suffer.

They might not understand or appreciate what she was about to do, but that didn't mean it wasn't the right thing to do. She gave herself a final once over and headed out the door.

~ ~

Damien looked over at his phone as it beeped. He arched an eyebrow as a text message came through from Zhara. He grinned. Apparently, she'd discovered the message he'd left her and was ready to make up with him.

He had no intention of meeting her anywhere. But it would be plenty of fun to watch her dance to his tune. He sent her an address to a rest stop a mile away from where he was staying in the hotel room.

He would make sure she sincerely regretted everything she'd done to him before he ever let her near him again. He wanted to see just how far she would go to prove to him that she was sorry. He wanted to see her on her knees, begging for mercy.

Only once she was completely and thoroughly humiliated would he even consider allowing her back into his bed. She was right that this was all her fault.

However, forgiveness was not on his agenda. She needed to pay for what she'd done to him. He needed to be sure he had enough leverage built up against her that she would never, even have the power to hurt him again. He wanted to be sure that once she was back in his life, she was going to stay for good.

Fortunately, he had all afternoon to plan out what he was going to do to her. He switched off the television and began whistling to himself as he got to work. By the time he was done with Zhara, she would have nowhere left to go except to beg for a place with him.

He would make her destroy every relationship she had with anyone else until there was nothing left in her world but him. And he would start with her relationship with her new boyfriend. He would make sure she was the one who poured the gasoline on that relationship and lit the fire. It would burn until there was nothing left of it.

Once she was done with that man, he would turn Mike and Gabby against her. She would cry and she would beg, but he knew that she would do anything to protect those two. And it was her very love for them and her desire to protect them that would allow him to manipulate her into betraying their trust and ruining their relationship.

She thought she could just leave him behind like some discarded piece of trash. She would learn, though. He would make sure that she understood her place. By the time he was done with her, she would never even think about leaving him again. There would be nowhere else for her to go.

Chapter 16

Gabby woke with a cry. Her bed was soaked in sweat. She could hear Damien's voice ringing in her ears, feel him unbuttoning her blouse. Adrenaline rushed through her veins.

She looked around and forced herself to relax. He wasn't here. She was safe. She was in her own bedroom. She was home.

Except that part of her wasn't. Part of her hadn't left that bunker. Part of her still felt helpless. Part of her kept wondering when he would strike again. The police had interviewed her, but she knew they hadn't found him yet.

She got out of bed and took a shower, trying to scrub the feel of him off of her skin. She scrubbed and scrubbed until her skin was red and raw, but it was never enough. No matter how much soap she applied, she could still feel him touching her. She got dressed and sat staring out the window.

She was angry. Damien stole her life. He stole her sense of security from her. He stole her peace of mind. He would have stolen her virginity, too, if she hadn't thought to lie to him. That was the only part of her past life that was still intact.

She wanted her life back. She wanted to feel safe and secure in her world again. She wanted to be able to sleep without dreaming of him and wake without thinking of him.

But she couldn't do that anymore. He filled her dreams when she lay down at night and her thoughts when she woke up each day. He was more in control of her than he'd ever been when she was in the bunker.

Mike had always been able to make her feel safe before this, but Mike hadn't been able to protect her from Damien when he'd kidnapped her. Mike hadn't been able to stop Damien from dragging her into that underground bunker and holding her there. He hadn't been able to stop Damien from any of it.

Worse, he kept telling her it was over. That she was safe now. But she didn't feel safe. She didn't feel like it was over. She would never feel safe as long as Damien was out there.

She'd never liked Damien, but she'd never hated him. She'd never hated anyone. All she'd wanted was for him to leave Zhara alone or at least stop breaking the kid's heart. She hated him now. She hated him with every fiber of her being.

She wanted to hurt him. She wanted to destroy him the way he'd destroyed her. She wanted him to feel every ounce of the pain that he'd caused her. If she couldn't get her life back, he shouldn't be free to live his.

Ironically, the hate made her feel more powerful. The hate made her feel capable of doing something about the situation. Maybe hate was an underrated emotion.

~ ~

Mike looked up from where he was polishing the bar. It was still hours until Purgatory opened, but he couldn't help himself. Cleaning made him feel like he was useful. Cleaning made him feel like he was in control of things. Those were two things he didn't find himself feeling very often lately.

There was a knock on the door and Mike threw the bar rag over his shoulder and headed toward the door. He was hoping it was the police come to tell him that they'd finally captured Damien so this could all be over. "John! What are you doing here?"

John shifted on his feet and gave a thin, small smile but there was a sadness in his eyes that was untouched by it. "I hoped you might be able to tell me where Zhara is. I tried to call her and sent her a text message, but I haven't heard from her. I am concerned about her."

Mike opened the door. "Come on in. I'll pour you a drink. To be honest, I haven't heard from her either."

John removed his fedora before stepping across the bar's threshold. Mike turned and headed back behind the bar. He didn't wait to see if John followed. "Not hearing from her doesn't concern you?"

Mike was startled by the question. He'd gotten used to long periods of Zhara not calling or coming by. Maybe John didn't know her that well. "Not really. Zhara's always been like that. She disappears and goes wherever she wants, and then she reappears eventually. I guess I just figured she'd come around when she was ready to talk and she's not ready yet."

John took a seat at the bar and set his fedora next to him. "And how is Gabriella?"

Mike frowned as he began cleaning the bar's surface again. "Quiet. Withdrawn."

John nodded. "Not at all like herself, is she?"

Mike stopped cleaning for a moment and gripped the towel harder. "No. Not at all like herself."

John hesitated for a moment and then spoke. "If I might offer a suggestion, try to remember that the Gabriella who was taken from the bar that night is not the same Gabriella that you see today. What has happened to her has changed her in ways even she isn't likely to recognize just yet. This may be over for you and for everyone else, but it's far from over for her. She may not act like she needs you right now, but she needs you more than ever."

Mike looked up. His words echoed some of the things that he'd heard Gabby say to him over the past few days. "How do you know?"

John frowned momentarily. "My mother was raped when I was 12 years old. She never saw the face of the man who did it. It was quite brutal. I was at school when the attacker struck. I found her when I got home. My parent's marriage was quite happy before that incident. But everything changed after that."

He paused for a moment and looked out the window, as if searching for something. "I think my father felt guilty for not being able to keep my mother safe. My mother may even, at least subconsciously, have blamed him for not being there to keep it from happening. He was in the military and stationed overseas. I think at least part of her believed that if he'd have just been home that day, it wouldn't have happened."

He turned his attention back to Michael. "Things fell apart quickly. I didn't understand what was happening, and I don't think my father did, either. My mother was always such a social creature but she stopped going out. She stopped talking much. She stopped smiling.

It was as if time moved on for the rest of us, but her life stopped right then. She couldn't move forward with us. She took her own life when I was sixteen. It was devastating, but in retrospect I am grateful that it happened."

Mike's eyebrows rose clear to his forehead. He couldn't help but interrupt. "Grateful? For your mother's suicide? Wow. That's harsh!"

John shook his head and held up a hand. "You misunderstand me. I am grateful because as tragic as that whole incident was, it changed the entire direction of my life. I miss my mother terribly and I grieve her loss deeply, but it was because of her death that I received the help I needed to become the man I am today. My therapist introduced me to music as an outlet for my feelings, and I became a musician instead of another statistic. Losing a parent to suicide when you are a child or teen makes you three times more likely to commit suicide yourself. I beat the odds."

Mike nodded. "You and me both. How do I reach Gabby, though? All she does is push me away. She tells me I won't understand, that I don't understand."

John gave him a measured look. "Accept that you do not understand and cannot understand what she's been through. Accept that she can't just forget or move on, though she wants to do both. Our tendency as men is to want to fix things for them, to put them back together and make them work the same way they used to. You can't fix this. You can't restore Gabby to what she was. But you can help her to become something new. You can help her to become a stronger version of herself."

Mike crossed his arms over his chest. "How? How do I help her when she won't let me?"

John held his gaze. "You teach her to take her pain and turn it into a gift that she uses to improve other people's lives. That's what I did with mine. I pour my pain into my music and that music then becomes a medium that helps people to express themselves and to find joy in their sorrows. Pain can destroy us or pain can become a path to build up the people around us."

John picked up his hat and gave Mike a sincere smile. "We don't get to choose the pain that we experience in life. It comes without our asking for it or wanting it. Our only choice, the only thing we get to decide in this life, is what we are going to do with the pain we've received."

Mike took a moment to consider John's words. "Thanks for the advice, man. I'll definitely take it under consideration."

John took a card out of his breast pocket and passed it across the table. "If you are interested, you and Gabby would be welcome at one of my concerts. I know it probably isn't the kind of thing you normally would attend, but I think you would find it meaningful."

Chapter 17

Zhara arrived at the address and frowned. It was a rest stop. Picnic tables were scattered among the trees. A cinder block building sporting bathrooms for men and women, divided by a huge state map in the center, was the dominant feature of the landscape. The area around the bathrooms was lit up with fluorescent lighting. The area around the picnic tables was dark.

She didn't see Damien's motorcycle anywhere. She looked at her cell phone. It was still 15 minutes until their arranged meeting. She paced out front of the rest area, stretching her legs and keeping a watch for his arrival. She felt nervous and jittery, almost like a first date. Except it was a date with death – hers or Damien's, only time would tell.

Time ticked by slowly. She found herself checking her phone every few minutes, waiting for the moment he would arrive, waiting for the moment she would have her chance to put an end to all of this. She wanted to head over to the picnic tables and wait there, but she wanted to be sure he saw her. She didn't want to risk him thinking she hadn't come.

Her stomach churned as she continued to pace. Cars came and went. This seemed to be a pretty busy stop along the way. It was less than ideal for what she had planned. She would have to convince Damien to go somewhere more private.

Fifteen minutes after the hour, there was still no sign of Damien. She began to get a bad feeling about this. Maybe Damien wasn't coming. Maybe he was just playing with her. She considered heading home. She decided she couldn't risk it. If there was even a chance that Damien would post those pictures on the internet and she could stop it, she would do what she could.

Thirty minutes after the hour and still no Damien. Her stomach was in knots. She sent a text message to Damien. "Where are you? I'm here."

There was no response. She hated this. Damien was still controlling her life, still forcing her to dance to his tune. Every time she thought she'd gotten the better of him, he'd found a way to come out on top. A sense of hopeless frustration welled up inside her but she quickly squished it back down. She reminded herself of the small package inside her purse. Things were going to end the way she wanted them to end for once.

~ ~

Damien watched her pacing through the binoculars and grinned. She'd never liked being kept waiting. All the more reason to make her wait now.

He heard the beep of his phone alerting him to a new text message and ignored it. She would get a response from him when he was good and ready to give it to her and not one moment before then.

At exactly one hour after he'd told her to meet him, he picked up the phone and dialed her number. He didn't even get through the first ring before she picked up. "Where are you?"

He smiled as he heard the frustration and impatience in her voice. "Where I am is not important. What is important is that you do exactly what I tell you to do. I am watching you. I will know if you don't."

There was a note of pleading in her voice that pleased him to no end when she finally responded. "Please, Damien. I'll do whatever you want. Just tell me what I have to do."

He laughed. "I want you to walk over to the picnic area. Underneath one of the tables is a box that has your name on it. Open it up and call me back. I'll tell you what to do next."

He hung up and watched with satisfaction as she made her way over to the picnic tables. It took her a little while to find the little box he'd hidden for her. It was gift wrapped. He watched as she opened it.

He knew exactly what she would find in that box. It was a steel choker with a lock. It was designed to look ornamental to the casual observer. He watched as she picked up the phone and called him. "I opened it. What do you want me to do now?"

He grinned. "I want you to put it on and be sure you snap that lock into place. However, before you do that, I am going to explain to you what it is and what it does so you know exactly what you are agreeing to before you do it. I don't want you saying I tricked you or forced you into this. You're going to make a choice tonight. You are going to trade Gabby's freedom for your own."

He paused and waited for her. "I'm listening."

He chuckled. "I'll just bet you are. That little piece of jewelry is a wearable cell phone. The front jewel hides the lens of a camera. There's a two-way microphone and a GPS tracking device embedded in it. Once you put it on and the lock snaps into place, the unit is activated and will begin transmitting signals to the app on my phone.

He paused to let that sink in before continuing. "The app will allow me to track your every movement. I can switch on that camera whenever I want and see whatever it is you are doing. I can listen in on any conversation you have at any time. I can use it to call you and give you commands. I will know if you obey those commands. There will be nowhere you can go that I can't find you."

The thought of having her completely under his control was intoxicating. He forced himself not to sound too eager. "I am the only one with a key to it. I am the only one who can remove it from around your neck once you put it on. Do this, and Gabby will be free. Nobody will ever find out about those photos. You will, however, belong to me. Do you understand?"

There was a pause on the other end of the line. Her voice was shaking when she finally answered him. "How can I be sure that you'll leave Gabby alone?"

Her question irritated him. "You can't. You can be sure I'll be posting those photos all over the internet if you choose not to do it. I don't care either way. Make a decision. I haven't got all night."

He watched as she picked up the choker and snapped the lock into place around her neck. "Just remember you gave yourself to me. I didn't force you to do it. No matter what happens, you have only yourself to blame."

~ ~

Zhara's stomach dropped and her hands shook as she snapped the collar into place around her neck. She tried to reassure herself that this was just part of getting close enough to Damien to destroy him.

It didn't matter what else happened. All that mattered was keeping the people she loved safe. The only way to keep them safe was to do whatever it took to earn Damien's trust. If that meant surrendering her freedom or even her life, so be it. "What do you want me to do now?"

His laughter sounded in her ears. She shivered slightly as a cold breeze began to blow. "Stop by my house. Leave your cell phone in my mail box. You won't be needing it any longer. If I want you to call someone, I'll call them for you. Then go home and wait for me. Leave your door unlocked. Don't answer the door, don't speak to anyone, and don't go anywhere without asking my permission first. Is that understood?"

A knife's edge of panic was rising in her. Somehow this was all going sideways. Control over the situation was slipping through her fingers and she didn't know how to get it back. His voice interrupted her thoughts. It was impatient, bordering on angry. "I asked a question. I expect an answer."

Her mouth was too dry to speak. She forced herself to swallow. She felt sick at her stomach. "Yes. I understand."

He sounded triumphant. "Good. Very good. Now, switch off your cell phone and go. Your new life begins right now."

With those words, he disconnected the call. She looked down at her cell phone, gritted her teeth, and turned it off. She strode over to her bike and got on. There was no turning back now.

She sped off down the road toward Damien's. She sat in front of his mail box as she pulled out her phone. She hesitated for a moment. She knew that once she put the cell phone in there, she was saying goodbye to her last and only lifeline. From this point forward, she would have no choice but to kill him if she ever hoped to be free.

There was a temptation to text John, to let him know that she was sorry, but she was afraid Damien would find out. There was no way for her to know when or if he was watching. She couldn't afford to have him question her loyalty or her obedience.

She pulled open the mailbox and slid the phone inside, then turned around and headed back up the street toward her apartment. She arrived home and climbed off her bike. She ran her hands along her grandfather's gun, still tethered to the side of the bike.

Her palms began to sweat and her heart pounded. If Damien was watching her, he would know that she had it. He might publish those photos of Gabby before she could stop him. But if he wasn't watching, she might be able to end this for once and for all. He'd ordered her to leave the door unlocked. It was plain that he intended to come over and pay her a visit. She could easily claim self-defense. She'd be the only one to know the truth.

Chapter 18

John looked at the address in his phone as he was driving slowly down the street. He was mentally preparing himself for what he was going to say to Zhara when he knocked on the door. He wasn't expecting to spot her in the driveway, standing beside her motorcycle.

He swung into an empty parking space and got out of the car. She was staring down at something and hadn't even looked up. "Zhara? Are you alright?"

She looked up at him and there was this incredibly guilty expression on her face, like a child whose hand was caught in a cookie jar. She didn't say anything to him, though. She just turned on her heel and walked back into the apartment building.

He followed after her. "Have I done something to upset you?"

She ran up the stairs and he quickened his pace to keep up with her. "Zhara, please. Talk to me. I can help you."

She got to the top of the stairs and opened her apartment door. Her eyes connected with his. This time they looked remarkably sad. She shook her head briefly before unlocking the door and stepping inside. She closed the door before he could come closer.

"Zhara, I know you've been through a lot. You don't have to deal with this alone. Just let me in. Whatever it is you're facing, I can help you."

He was met with more silence. It absolutely baffled him. He could not understand her behavior. Just a day and a half ago, she was clinging to him as if her life depended upon it. Today, she wouldn't even speak to him.

"Whatever it is you're hiding from me, Zhara, I will find out. Please don't shut me out like this. I want to help you." Still there was only silence.

He sighed heavily and turned to walk back down the steps. "I do love you, Zhara. I want you to know that nothing you can do or have done will ever change that. Loving you is a choice I made, and there is nothing you can do that will cause me to choose otherwise."

His heart ached but the last thing he wanted was to force himself on her. If she truly didn't want him there, he wouldn't make her let him into her life.

He walked out into the night and opened up the passenger door, looking up at Zhara's window. The light was on and she was clearly visible from the street.

It was evident to him that she was watching him. Her hand was pressed against the window, open palmed. It was gesture totally at odds with her earlier behavior.

"Do not leave her." The still, small voice was barely a whisper but it was clear.

He knew this voice far too well to ignore it. Zhara needed him whether she was ready to admit it or not. He slipped back into his car as if he were leaving but kept his eyes focused on her window.

~ ~

Zhara was about to remove the gun from its tether when she heard John's voice. Startled, she turned to see him walking toward her. She felt immediately guilty for everything she'd been thinking of doing to Damien.

She also felt panic. She'd taken enough risks tonight. She couldn't afford to take more. Damien had ordered her not to speak to anyone.

She turned on her heel and headed for the apartment. John followed her. He was begging her to talk to him. Everything inside of her wanted to talk to him, to open up to him and let him in, to take refuge in his arms.

But that was a lie. He couldn't defend her or protect her from Damien. No one could. Only death could stop Damien. And the only way she would have a chance of stopping Damien was to obey his commands. Which meant she had to ignore John.

She hesitated for a moment before opening her door and looked at him for the first time. She knew once she went inside the door, nothing would ever be the same for either of them. This would have to be goodbye. A man like John didn't deserve to be drug into all of this.

She closed the door behind her and sank down against it, curling her knees against her chest and burying her face. Her heart ached as his words tugged at her heart.

"Loving you is a choice I made, and there is nothing you can do that will cause me to choose otherwise."

She mouthed the words she didn't dare to speak aloud. "I love you, too, John."

His footsteps faded and she rose and walked over to the window. Her eyes followed him all the way to his car. She pressed the palm of her hand against the window as if she could somehow touch him that way. She watched him get into his car and turned away. She couldn't stand watching him leave.

Maybe, when this was all over, she would be able to explain things to him. Maybe he would understand why she'd done what she was going to do. She knew she didn't deserve him. Would he still choose to love her when he discovered the truth about who she was? Would he still choose to love her when she had Damien's blood on her hands?

She was fairly certain she knew the answer to that question. What man in his right mind would want her?

~ ~

Damien couldn't believe how easy it had been to get Zhara to put that collar around her neck. He'd promised himself that he wouldn't take her back into his bed until she was thoroughly humiliated and begging him for mercy. That collar was the first step in making sure that every part of his plan came together.

The next step was waiting for him in Zhara's apartment. He checked the app to be sure she was still there. She hadn't moved in the last hour. He switched on her camera and microphone.

She was curled up on the couch in the living room watching television. She was all alone. He switched it off, content with knowing that she was exactly where she ought to be. He gunned his bike and pulled out of his hiding spot, heading down the highway.

Her street was completely dark when he arrived with the exception of a few scattered street lights that were so weak they might as well not have been there at all. Long shadows stretched in every direction. The lights were all off in Zhara's apartment. He paused to switch on the camera and the microphone. She'd moved into her bed and appeared to be sleeping.

He reached into the saddlebags of his bike and pulled out a few zip ties and tucked them into his belt loops. He also pulled out the usb charger, which was shaped like a leash, just in case the collar began running low before the sun could recharge its batteries.

He slipped down the sidewalk and up the stairs to Zhara's apartment. He tested the door knob. She'd left it unlocked just as he had ordered her to do. He slipped inside and made his way to her bedroom. She was sound asleep.

He slid the covers back and shook her. Her eyes opened and widened as she saw him.

"Damien."

He put a finger to her lips. "Remember our agreement."

He tapped the collar around her neck. "You belong to me. Is that understood?"

She nodded her head. He put a finger under her chin and lifted her face, looking her in the eyes. He caressed her hair for a moment. "Get on your knees and beg me for permission to show me you mean it."

She swallowed, but got on her knees without a single word of protest. "Please, Damien. Please let me show you that I belong to you."

He took the ring off his finger and wrapped the smooth part of the ring with leather before handing it to her and then pulled a lighter out of his pocket.

He flicked it and the flames began to dance. "You want to show me that you belong to me? You want a chance to prove you mean it? This is your chance. I want you to brand yourself with my ring."

She opened her mouth to protest but shut it. She nodded her head.

"Hold the ring over this flame until the timer goes off. Then, press that ring right here."

He tapped to a spot right at the cleft between her breasts. "I want every man who sees you to know whose property you are."

. She held the ring over the flame until the timer went off and gritted her teeth before moving the ring to the cleft and pressing it as hard against her skin as hard as she could.

Her hands shook and he put his hand over hers to be sure she was pressing it against her skin as hard as the bone would allow. Tears welled up in her eyes and flowed down her cheeks, but she didn't let go.

The second timer went off and he reclaimed his ring. It was still warm but no longer hot enough to burn. He moved a finger around the mark on her flesh. She flinched but didn't pull back. "Thank me for making you mine."

She locked eyes with him. Her eyes were red-rimmed but the flow of tears had stopped. "Thank you for making me yours."

He grinned and stood over her. "Now, show me how grateful you are to be mine."

Chapter 19

John looked over as the noise of a motorcycle rumbling into the parking lot caught his attention. He frowned as the figure, clearly visible in the light cast from the headlight, turned off the engine and climbed off the bike. Darkness was restored as he stalked toward Zhara's apartment.

"Damien." John wasn't expecting this. He was concerned for her safety and picked up his cell phone, quickly dialing 9-1-1.

"9-1-1 what is the nature of the emergency?"

He gripped the phone tightly as he opened his car door. "I just witnessed the man who kidnapped my friend heading toward her apartment."

The operator sounded slightly confused. "I'm sorry. Can you repeat that?"

John grimaced as he tried to both stay out of Damien's sight and deal with the operator at the same time. He didn't want to alert Damien to the fact that the police were being called and risk having him escape before they could get there.

"The man who kidnapped my friend is heading toward her apartment. His name is Damien McKnight. Please dispatch the police immediately."

"What's the address, sir?"

John felt annoyed. The operator didn't seem to understand the gravity of the situation. "The apartment is at 13 Cherrycreek Drive, number 2111. Please hurry. I am concerned for her safety."

The operator's voice didn't change. "I understand your concern, sir. I am working as quickly as I can to get the information I need so I can call it into dispatch."

He tried to keep his voice low as he crept closer to the building. "What more do you need? I've given you all the relevant information."

He opened the door gingerly and stared up the darkened stairwell. He wasn't sure what he expected to hear, but there didn't seem to be any noise coming from her apartment.

"I am calling in your report to the police as we speak. However, I will need you to stay on the line with me until they arrive."

He rolled his eyes. He crept up the staircase. He could hear his heart pounding in his ears. He was terrified for Zhara. "Did they say how long until they can get here?"

As expected, the operator's next words did nothing to reassure him. "I'm afraid not, sir. You'll just need to be patient."

His jaw clenched, but he forced himself to remain polite. Rudeness would get him nowhere, and it wasn't the operator's fault.

"I see." He hated the fact that Zhara hadn't let him in tonight. He hated the fact that he was forced to remain on the outside while she tried to battle Damien on her own.

He could hear voices inside her apartment but it was impossible to make out what was being said. Not for the first time, he wished she would just open up the door and let him in already. This time, preferably, literally.

"Sir, are you there?"

He'd been so intent on Zhara's apartment that he had forgotten he was on the phone. "I am."

The operator was trying to be reassuring, but came off as merely irritating. "Things are going to be fine, sir. The police should be there any minute. Where are you now, sir?"

John sighed. He had a feeling he was about to be told to stay out of the way. "I'm standing in front of her apartment."

The operator paused a moment. "The police have asked that you get a safe distance away. Can you do that?"

Could he physically do that? Almost certainly. Could he do that emotionally? It seemed an impossibility. Zhara needed him whether she would admit that to him or not.

Still, he did not want to cause problems for the police or slow them down because of him. "I will do that." He returned to his car to wait for whatever might come next.

The police pulled up in a squad car a few minutes later and proceeded into the building.

~ ~

There was a pounding on the front door. Zhara jumped at the sound.

"Open up. This is the police."

Damien swore and his eyes narrowed dangerously as he stared down at her. She tensed as they pounded on the door again.

His voice was a low growl. "You tell them anything and I swear to you that I will make your life a living hell. Go answer that damn door."

She got up off the floor without a backwards look, pulling her clothes together as she went. "Coming."

She tried to keep her voice even, but she was shaking as she opened the front door just a crack.

"Ma'm, we had a report that Damien McKnight was seen in this area. Has he paid you a visit?"

Years of practice lying to protect herself came to her rescue in that moment. She was able to look him in the eyes. "I don't know where he is."

The man gave her a brief, but friendly, smile and wrote something down on his notepad. "Do you mind if I come in and look around? The caller seemed pretty concerned about your safety and pretty certain that Damien was in this area. The case file did say that the two of you had a previous relationship…"

She forced a smile on her face. "If you really think it's necessary, Officer…"

He tapped the badge on his shirt. "Henderson. Detective Henderson, actually. You know that Damien is a wanted man, right? Anyone caught harboring him could face some serious jail time. I promise you I won't take long. Just long enough to make sure you're not in any danger."

She opened the door and let him inside. She frowned and crossed her arms over her chest as she watched him work. Her heart pounded in her chest.

A few minutes later, he called out to her from her bedroom. "Do you always leave your balcony door open at night, Miss?"

She felt her cheeks flushing. Damien must have fled. "Only when it's too hot for me to sleep."

He stepped back into the front room and handed her a business card. "Are you sure that's wise? If you do see Damien, be sure to give me a call. It doesn't matter what time it is."

She looked at the card. It read, "Detective Anthony Henderson."

"Detective, I promise I will call you if there's anything to report. In the meantime, I'd like to go back to bed."

He locked eyes with her for a half a second more than was comfortable. She forced herself to hold his gaze without blinking. The smile returned, this time accompanied by a dimple in the right cheek. "I hope to hear from you soon."

With that, he walked out her door and shut it gently behind him. She waited until he was gone to return to the bedroom. Sure enough, Damien was gone. He'd left without a trace. She was both relieved and even more scared than she had been.

She looked down at the parking lot, looking for Damien's bike. It was nowhere to be seen. But what was to be seen was John's car.

Her heart sank. John knew that Damien had been here, and now he would know that she'd lied about not having seen Damien. She couldn't tell him the truth about why she'd done it, either.

If Damien found out that she'd betrayed him, there was no telling what he might do to her. He was not going to let her go, that was for certain.

However, if she didn't tell John the truth, and the police questioned him, they would find out she'd lied. She could be in serious trouble. She could be arrested.

She didn't know what to do now. Things were going from bad to worse and there didn't seem any way to make things better. She needed to get away, but there was nowhere for her to go that Damien couldn't find her.

~ ~

John watched in disbelief as the policeman left without Damien. For the first time, he considered the possibility that maybe the other night's kidnapping hadn't been enough for Zhara to break off her relationship with Damien. Maybe she just wasn't ready to let him go in spite of all he'd done to her, to Gabby, and to Mike.

Maybe it was time for him to face the fact that she didn't want to be with him. She wanted to be with Damien. A part of him said, "Let her go." The other part of him said, "There's got to be an explanation for all this!"

He shook his head. It was time to stop excusing Zhara. She was not a child. She was a 22-year-old woman with a mind of her own. It was also time for him to face up to the facts. Time after time, she'd continued to choose Damien over him. As much as he wanted things to be different, that was the reality. Perhaps it was time he respect what were clearly her wishes.

He couldn't save Zhara from herself. However, that didn't mean he needed to leave Mike and Gabby vulnerable to Damien. He needed to warn them about Damien.

It was only fair to the two of them. Zhara made her choice. It was time they be given that same chance to make theirs.

He started to back out of the driveway, but his heart wouldn't let him leave yet. He'd told her that he'd made a choice to love her regardless of whether she ever learned to love him in return. He meant that. He wanted her to know that if she ever changed her mind and decided that she wanted something better for herself, he would be waiting for her.

It took him over an hour, and a half of a spiral notebook, to put into words the way that he felt. It wasn't easy to get his emotions down on paper in a way that satisfied him, but he finally did. He climbed the stairs one final time and hesitated at her door.

He knew that once he put the note under the door, this was likely to be it for the two of them. He stared at the letter for the longest time before he finally gathered up his resolve and slid the papers under the door. Then he turned and walked back into the night, wiping away the tears as he went.

Chapter 20

Zhara stood by the door, her hand on it as if to reach through and touch John, listening as his footsteps paused outside. She wanted to open the door for him, to let him in, to beg him to stay, but she couldn't. Gabby's life for hers. That had been the deal. She couldn't afford for Damien to catch her breaking the deal, no matter how much pain it caused her.

After what seemed an eternity of silence, she saw a stack of folded papers slide beneath the door and reached down to pick them up. Her heart broke as she read the words on the page.

"*My beloved Zhara,*

I told you once that my love for you is no mere feeling, but a choice that I have made. There is nothing that you can do that will change my decision.

For love to be real, it must be an act of the will, fully and freely chosen. So as hard as it is for me to understand your reasons for choosing Damien, I respect you enough to honor the choice you've made. I won't force my attentions on you.

Know that if ever you should change your mind, you

have only to call upon me. I promise you that no matter the time of day or the distance between us, I will come for you.

Yours, always and forever,

John"

Tears formed in her eyes as she heard his footsteps turn and walk slowly back down the steps. She knew that she could stop him from leaving. All she would have to do is open the door and call his name. Instead, she put her head in her hands and sank down to the floor, leaning against the solid wood for support.

She allowed the tears to flow this time but choked back the sobs. She didn't want to chance Damien hearing them or knowing that he'd wounded her. If he was watching, she wanted him to think that everything was fine between the two of them.

She wiped the tears from her eyes and stared at the letter. John was too good to her and too good for her. She'd never deserved him and didn't now. As much as his leaving hurt, it was almost a relief. She couldn't hurt him anymore. He would be free to find someone who would make him happy in ways that she never could.

It was Damien's fault that she'd lost him, though. It was Damien who had forced her into a position where she couldn't explain things to John without betraying Gabby, and that was something she would never do. Not after everything that Mike and Gabby had done for her.

She scowled as she thought about everything that Damien had done to her in these last few weeks. He'd destroyed her relationship with John. He'd threatened Gabby's life and then her reputation. He'd stolen her freedom.

She stood up and opened the door, heading down the stairs and moving toward her bike. The next time that Damien paid her a visit, he was going to meet more than Zhara.

He was going to find himself on the business end of her grandfather's rifle. She was going to make good and sure that Damien never stole anything else from her or the people she loved ever again.

~ ~

Tony Henderson pulled into the parking lot of Purgatory. He glanced at his notebook. Gabriella and Michael Montrose were the primary complainants against Damien McKnight. He was hopeful that they could provide him additional information about the connection between Damien and Zhara Wahlinski.

He'd found no evidence in the apartment to prove that Zhara was lying to him, but everything in his gut told him that she was. What he didn't know for sure was why.

He pushed open the door and stepped inside to find his ears assaulted with the loud music. He made his way through the crowd and stepped up to the bar. Michael smiled at him as he spotted him.

"Detective Henderson. You off duty or on?"

Tony nodded.

"On duty, I'm afraid. Is your sister available? I need to ask her some questions about the case."

Michael's smile disappeared. He pointed to a table in the back corner where the red head was busy serving drinks to a couple of bikers. Tony waded through more crowds to reach her.

"Ms. Montrose, I don't know if you remember me. I'm Detective Anthony Henderson. I need to ask you a few questions about the case."

She pursed her lips together before she tucked her empty tray beneath her arm and nodded, then gestured toward a small hallway. "The office is back there. It'll be a lot quieter."

He followed along behind her until they reached the office. She unlocked the door and led him inside, then gestured toward a seat in front of the desk while she took the one behind it. "Ask away."

Her grey eyes settled on his.

"Ms. Montrose…"

She interrupted him. "Call me Gabby, please."

He looked up and smiled. "Yes, ma'm. I'll keep that in mind. What I was going to say is can you tell me a little bit about the relationship between Ms. Walinski and Mr. McKnight? Someone reported seeing him entering her apartment building but I didn't find him when I got there."

He watched her face closely as he said those words, trying to gauge her reaction. There was clear evidence of surprise and a trace of anger that immediately followed. What he didn't know for sure was the source of the anger.

"Zhara and Damien have been together on and off since she was 16 years old. They break up about every six weeks like clockwork only to get back together again when the dust has settled. I never liked the relationship, but there was not a whole lot that I could do about it."

She shrugged. "He didn't seem to be outright breaking the law or physically abusing her, so there wasn't anything I could do. Then, about three months ago, things changed. Zhara met somebody new. I don't know why this guy was different or what set him off, but Damien went nuts. He just went nuts."

He could tell that Gabby wanted to say more. She opened her mouth, but then thought better of it and said nothing. He allowed silence to build between them, hoping she would feel uncomfortable enough to talk.

She frowned. "Of all the men in a 5 mile radius that Zhara could have picked, I don't know why she chose Damien. And, honestly, if you're wondering if she helped him escape, I don't know. Under normal circumstances, I would swear to you that she'd never do anything to help someone who hurt me and Mike like that. But nothing to do with Damien's been normal."

He leaned back in his seat and listened. Gabby glanced at him briefly and then down at the desk. "She was willing to do anything,"

Her voice grew husky and she didn't look up. "Allow him to do anything to her to protect me in that bunker. I think if he'd told her she had to kill herself to save me, she would have. If she's protecting Damien, after what he did to me, it's a sure bet that it's because he's convinced her that he can somehow get to me and hurt me if she doesn't."

She locked eyes with him and he could see the tears pooling in the corners. "Damien's got his hooks in my little sister and he's bound and determined not to let her go. I think you're honestly the only one who can help her right now. Please, Detective, make her talk to you. Make her tell you whatever it is that he's using against her. Lock her up if you have to, but make her do it."

Tony wondered how much of her statement was the truth and how much of it was her being in denial about Zhara's role in all of this. "I've met a lot of women who are with abusers. Most of them protect the men who abuse them, even when those men are hurting their kids or other people they love. What makes you think Zhara's different?"

Gabby hesitated and sighed. "When Damien kidnapped me, Zhara was safe. She was hiding out from him in a place he would never find her – and she knew that. She didn't have to come back. She knew she was putting herself in danger by coming for me when she found out what he'd done. None of us knew exactly what Damien would do, either to her or to me, but she loved me enough to risk everything."

Gabby angrily rubbed tears from her cheeks. Her copper hair framed her face in a red-gold halo but those grey eyes of hers grew dark like a stormy sea. Her voice caught for a moment. "If she's in trouble, it's my fault. She wouldn't be in this situation if it weren't for me. Please, Detective. I'm begging you. Help her. Do whatever you have to do, but help her get free of Damien."

Tony put on his best poker face. As much as there was a part of him that wanted to promise whatever it would take to wipe those tears from her eyes, the professional in him knew better. "Thank you for speaking with me tonight, Ms. Montrose. I can certainly understand your concerns. I assure you that I will do whatever I can, but as for helping Ms. Walinski, that's going to depend on her. I can't help someone who doesn't want to be helped, no matter how well intentioned."

Chapter 21

"You hungry?"

A large pair of amber eyes stared out of a too-thin face from beneath the bleachers. The child's dark, curly hair was matted and her face was filthy.

She eyed Mike with suspicion but her hand darted out to grab hold of the bag he passed her. Mike sat down on a deserted seat and watched her tear into the food like a hungry wolf. "You have a name?"

The girl's mouth was crammed so full of sandwich her cheeks were bulging. She reminded him of a squirrel. He smothered a grin. She glanced over at him and shook her head.

"No Name it is, then. Well, No Name, if you happen to be interested in a warm place to sleep tonight, you could just follow me. I happen to know of a place where the door's always unlocked." He looked at his watch. Gabby would be finished with drama practice soon. The two of them always walked home together. Ten minutes later, he watched her emerge from the drama hall and begin the climb to the stadium.

Fall leaves crunched beneath their feet as the twins left the high school behind. He could hear a smaller crunch behind them and winked at Gabby. "How was practice today?"

Gabby swept a hand to her forehead and feigned wiping her brow with a dramatic flourish. Her voice took on a noticeable Southern drawl. "As Gawd iz mah witness, I weel nevuh bee hungreh ah-gayhn!"

She grinned at Mike and her voice returned to normal. "I think I'm getting the hang of it"

He laughed and shook his head. "It doesn't surprise me you like playing Scarlett O'Hara. She's the ultimate drama queen. You two have a lot in common."

Gabby dropped a quick courtesy aimed in Mike's direction. "Correction! I'm not a drama queen. I am THE drama queen!! Bow before me!"

He mock bowed before her and caught a glimpse of a dark curly head lurking in the shadows behind them. He pretended not to see her. "I stand corrected."

The two of them lapsed into a comfortable silence born from long years together. Gabby was the first one to break it. "Any more word from the Marine recruiter?"

Mike kicked a pebble in the road. "I heard from him today, actually. They got my test results back. It looks good. They are getting the early entry program paperwork ready. If Grandpa agrees to sign it, I'll start daily PT after school."

Gabby looked at him, her brows furrowed with concern, and a frown settled over her face. "You sure this is what you want? There are other ways to pay for college, you know."

Mike put a reassuring arm around her shoulders. "I'm not just doing it for college. I want to serve my country. I want to know that I am defending the people I love the most."

Gabby nodded, but the frown didn't ease from her face. "I guess. I just wish you didn't have to leave us behind to do it."

He shook his head. "I wish I didn't have to leave, too, but the honest truth is that I want to see more of the world. I love the bar and I love Grandpa, but there's way more to life than this. Besides, you're planning to head off to UNR once we graduate. You're not sticking around anymore than I am."

Gabby looked up at Mike and locked eyes. He could see the fear in them. "I'll still be home on the weekends. You're going to be halfway around the world doing who knows what. I want you to be happy, but I don't have to like it."

He stopped and turned to her. "Gabby, just say the word and I won't go. You're more important to me than anything else. "

She shook her head and kept walking. "You know I'm not going to stop you from doing what you want to do. I love you. Even if you are a knucklehead."

He chuckled. "The term is jarhead."

She rolled her eyes. "Whatever. It still amounts to the same."

He caught up to her and they kept walking. He heard a third set of footsteps behind him and knew that the kid was still following behind them. They reached the turn off for Purgatory and headed around back to the set of stairs that led up to the living quarters above the bar. Mike winked at Gabby. "That No Name person might just want to head up these steps if she wanted to find that warm place to sleep I was telling you about earlier, Gabby."

Gabby smiled at him. "Yup. There might even be a few pillows and maybe some blankets there."

They climbed up the steps and left the door unlocked before hanging their school bags on the hooks in the mudroom. The smell of fried spiced potatoes and steak wafted through the air from the kitchen. The twins followed the scent.

Grandpa was standing at the stove. "Dinner will be ready in a few minutes. Mike, Gabby, set the table. Lay an extra plate in case we have a guest."

The twins got to work and had the table ready just as their grand-father was setting dishes of food in the center. Mike and Gabby took a seat and the three of them made the sign of the cross before Grandpa led them in a blessing over the food.

"Bless us, oh Lord, and these thy gifts, which we are about to re-ceive, from thy bounty, through Christ our Lord. Amen." Grandpa glanced at the figure lurking in the doorway.

His bushy eyebrows shot straight up to the place where his hairline used to be and then he glanced at Mike and Gabby. "You brought a friend home? Why did you not invite your friend to eat with us?"

Mike looked at his grandpa and shrugged. "No Name, would you like to come eat with us? I know you had that sandwich earlier but this is much better food."

The dark haired child stepped cautiously away from the doorway and slid into the empty seat. Grandpa crossed his arms over his chest.

"No Name, eh? We can't have that. You need a real name. What is your name?"

She looked down at her plate and frowned but looked back up at Grandpa and crossed her arms over her chest. "Zhara. My name is Zhara."

Grandpa nodded, taking the information in. "Well, Zhara, we have a few rules in this house you'll have to follow. First, if you're hungry, you eat. If you're thirsty, you drink. Don't bother to ask for permission. Just get what you need. Second, if you're going to stay here, you're going to be treated like family. Everyone who lives here works here. We all pitch in and we all do chores. Do you think you can handle that?"

Zhara hesitated for a moment and then nodded. "Yes, sir."

Grandpa crossed his arms over his chest and returned her nod. "Good enough."

After dinner, the four of them worked together to clean and put away the dishes before it was time to take baths. Gabby gave Zhara an old nightgown of hers to wear.

Gabby was short enough that on Zhara that the gown stopped just above her knees. "Goodness. Too much shorter and we'd have to make you a whole new gown!"

Gabby shook her head and grinned. "Well, you're definitely taller than I am. I do still have you beat in the chest department, but that might change in a few years. We'll have to see. At any rate, your bedroom is down the hall. Let us know if you need anything."

~ ~

Mike watched the detective head out of the bar. Gabby didn't return to serving drinks for quite a while after he left and her eyes were rimmed red when she finally did. He wondered what, exactly, the detective had said to his sister and made a note to talk to Gabby once the bar was closed.

This mess with Damien was killing him. He was a former Marine. He'd signed up to protect and serve but he couldn't protect the women he loved most. That didn't sit well with him.

He didn't have a lot of time to dwell on things, though. Tending the bar kept him busy most of the time. It was in his off hours that he felt the depression coming over him and struggled to fight against it. His depression was one of the few things he held back from Gabby as much as he possibly could. She had enough burdens to carry. She didn't need to carry his, too.

He'd joined the Marines to see the world, and he had. But the price he'd paid for seeing the world was seeing things he couldn't erase from his memory. He'd discovered a darker side to life than he'd ever imagined existed back when he was growing up.

He'd always had a sense of humor. It was what saved him. That sense of humor came because he'd spent so much time staring into the face of darkness that he'd discovered it had pimples and bad breath. The longer he stared, the funnier the darkness grew. There was a danger there, though, because sometimes when he least expected it, he would discover that the darkness was starting to swallow him. It got hard to tell where the darkness ended and he began. Those were the moments when he found himself feeling useless and worthless, wondering what was the point of him being alive if he couldn't save the people he loved the most by doing it.

Gabby and Zhara were usually the reasons that made life worth living. When he got to feeling like this, though, all he could see was his failure to be there for them and to protect them. He started to feel like their lives would be so much better without him.

When he was in the Marines, he could shoot the enemies that threatened the people he loved most. In the bar, he could throw out the people that were a threat to the people he loved. But when it came to Damien, his hands were tied. There was nothing he could do – at least, nothing legal.

Chapter 22

Damien swore as he walked into the motel room and slammed the door behind him. Where was he supposed to go now? He couldn't go back to his own house. He couldn't go back to Zhara's.

With that Detective having showed up at Zhara's, it was a good bet the cops were looking for him again. They were bound to find him if he stayed here too much longer.

His plans to blackmail Zhara and Gabby into silence were falling to pieces. He couldn't retrieve Zhara's cell phone from his mailbox. He couldn't risk delivering the photos to her in person.

He needed another plan. He needed a place to stay. Somewhere there wouldn't be any questions asked.

He picked up his cell phone and typed in a name. Rita Summers. A smile spread across his face. It'd been more than six months since he'd last seen her. It wouldn't matter, though.

Rita was a lot like a dog: loyal, faithful, always eager to see him, and never asking questions about where he'd been or why he'd been gone for so long. She was exactly who he needed right now.

He checked the time. It was 10:30 at night. For most people, that might have been too late. Rita was a night owl, though. She would still be up for a few hours. He dialed the number.

"Rita. Am I calling too late?" The smile in her voice told him everything he needed to know about the kind of welcome he could expect.

"Damien! You know it's never too late for you where I'm concerned. You planning to drop by? Luke's been asking about you. He sure does miss you."

Damien relaxed, feeling the tension leave his body, and a grin stretched across his face. "Yeah? Well, I've missed having my little buddy around, too. It'll be good to see him again. How about you? You missed me, too?"

Her voice lowered slightly and there was a hunger to it that he recognized. "Oh, I have missed you. It gets pretty lonely out here, especially at night."

Those words were exactly the ones he was hoping to hear. "I guess you wouldn't mind some company for a while, then?"

Barely disguised eagerness mingled with a hint of curiosity was in her voice as she replied. "I've told you before my door is always open for as long as you want to stay. It'd be nice to have some adult company around here. Besides, I wouldn't mind having a man around to help out. There's always plenty of work to be done on the ranch. I could use an extra pair of hands."

Damien frowned briefly at the thought of the never-ending ranch work, but he was running out of options. He forced a smile back on his face. "I just might know someone who'd be more than happy to lend you a pair of hands. Give me an hour to clean up and make my way out there."

She chuckled. "I'll leave the light on and the door unlocked. Can't wait to see you. It's been far, far too long."

Rita was waiting for him in a button down plaid shirt and not a whole lot else when he walked through the door. She stood up to greet him and he wrapped his arms around her waist and kissed her.

She curled her arms around his neck and laid her head against his chest. "Oh, God, I've missed that."

He didn't answer her. He just swept her up in his arms and carried her into the bedroom.

~ ~

Tony knocked on Zhara's door. "Ms. Walinksi. Open up. It's the police. I need to speak with you."

She opened the door much sooner than he anticipated. Her eyes were red-rimmed and her face was a bit splotchy. There was a scowl on her face. "I spoke with you earlier, didn't I?"

He ignored the irritation in her voice. "You did. However, I need to ask you some additional questions. I'm afraid I'll need you to come down to the station with me."

Her eyes widened momentarily. "Is that really necessary? Can't you just ask me here?"

He observed how tightly she was gripping the door. It was clear she was afraid of something. He needed to know what it was and why. "I'm afraid not. "

She pursed her lips. "Can I at least put some shoes on?"

She opened the door so he could step into the apartment.

"Yes. Be quick about it, though. And, Ms. Walinski, just in case you were thinking about leaving the same way Mr. McKnight did, I wouldn't recommend it."

She gave him a withering glance. "I'm not going to run, if that's what you're thinking."

He crossed his arms over his chest as she sat down and began putting her shoes on her feet. "I'm glad to hear that. I would hate to bring you into the precinct tired."

She looked up and there was a spark of something in her eyes. She clearly didn't like being challenged. "Believe me, Detective, if I wanted to run, you wouldn't find me."

He'd heard a lot of false bravado in his day. She sounded fairly confident in her statement, which made him curious. "What makes you think that?"

She stood up and headed toward the door without a backward glance in his direction. "Better men than you tried and failed."

He grinned. "No respect for the badge, hmm?"

She shook her head, sending the dark curls bouncing every direction. "In my experience, men who hide behind badges tend to be the kind who like power. They're also the kind who tend to abuse it."

He opened the cruiser back door and let her inside. "Guess it's your lucky day. I didn't get a badge for the power it gave me and I am not the kind who abuses it, either. "

He waited until she was seated and buckled before shutting the door after her. Zhara shrugged. "We'll see about that."

~ ~

Zhara sat in the back of the police car, her hand clenched into a fist, tears forming in her eyes. If Damien saw what was happening, this was it for Gabby. He would spread those nasty pictures all over the internet and there wouldn't be a thing she could do to protect her.

She suddenly felt tired, small, and hopeless. Once again, Damien was messing up her life. She felt like she would never be free of the man. And the collar she was wearing was a cold reminder of that.

The collar. How was she going to explain THAT to the detective? Should she just tell him the truth and get it over with?

Her stomach churned as she worked through the possibilities in her mind. They arrived at the station and Detective Henderson opened the door for her. She got out and walked into the station in front of him, then waited for him to direct her to the interrogation room.

He gestured toward a small room just around the corner, then closed the door after her. She took a seat on the opposite side of the table from him.

"Let's start from the beginning, Ms. Walinski. I arrived at your apartment based on a report that Damien McKnight was seen entering your apartment building. You claimed not to know where he was. You also claimed that you left your balcony door open because it was too hot for you to sleep. Do you wish to stick to that story or would you like to tell me what's really going on here?"

Zhara felt her face turning red, but she remained silent.

"Ms. Walinski. I would like to help you. Your –sister- Ms. Montrose, believes you are in some kind of trouble. She believes that Mr. McKnight is holding something over you. If that is the case, and you are honest with me, I can help you. Blackmail is a federal charge. If he is indeed engaging in blackmail, I can add that to his current list of charges and we can pursue him. Is she right? Is Mr. McKnight holding something over you?"

Her mind raced. Gabby knew. She didn't know how Gabby found out, but she knew the truth. A huge weight was lifted from her shoulders. John might not have understood, but Gabby knew her. Gabby understood.

She nodded, swallowed hard to clear her throat, and gathered up her courage. "He has pictures. Of Gabby."

She grimaced as she remembered the lurid image on her cell phone. She blinked back tears and she felt her throat tightening. "He said he would post them on the internet if I didn't do what he wanted."

The detective looked at her. "And what was it he wanted you to do, Ms. Walinski?"

She looked at the table. It was so hard to admit the truth. She felt like her face was on fire. She noticed a small carving in the steel table and traced her finger around it as she fought through the shame and the guilt to reach a place where she could bring herself to tell him.

"Ms. Walinski?"

She found herself desperately wishing that a giant hole would open up in the ground and swallow her whole, but no such mercy was given her. Finally, she forced herself to speak. "He made me put this collar on"

She tapped the silver collar around her neck. "So he could track me. He wanted me to trade my life for hers. He…"

Her fingers shook as she unbuttoned the top two buttons of her shirt to allow him to see the area where he'd ordered her to brand herself with his ring. "He kept…he kept saying he wanted to make sure I couldn't ever leave him. He wanted everybody to know who I…who I belonged to."

The tears that she'd fought so hard to keep back forced their way forward and she buried her face in her arm so he couldn't see them. Her shoulders shook as she tried to keep the sobs from escaping. The only noise in the room was her periodic gasps for breath.

The detective's voice was gentle, compassionate, but with a measure of control to it that covered a well of emotions. "Thank you for cooperating, Ms. Walinski. I know this hasn't been easy for you, but I assure you that you've done the right thing in being honest with me. I can assure you that I will do everything in my power to protect both you and Ms. Montrose from Mr. McKnight. I know you may find this hard to believe right now, but that collar around your neck may very well prove to be the key to setting both you and Ms. Montrose free of him for good."

Chapter 23

Tony passed Zhara a cup of coffee. "I need you to tell me everything that Mr. McKnight told you about what the collar did and how it works. "

She closed her eyes and took a sip of coffee. "He said it's like a cell phone. The gem on the front is like a camera. It can take pictures or record video. There's a microphone so he can listen and a transmitter so he can give me directions or whatever. And it has a GPS."

Tony nodded, keeping his poker face firmly in place, but he wanted to smile and do a happy dance. If this was transmitting signals to a cell phone, all they had to do was track where those signals were going and they would have Damien in their hands. "I see. How did Mr. McKnight inform you about his possession of the photographs of Ms. Montrose?"

Zhara looked down at the table again for a moment. "He sent one to me on my cell phone and told me that there were plenty more where that one came from."

Tony nodded. That was another positive, assuming they could retrieve her cell phone. "Where is your cell phone now?"

Zhara looked up at him and frowned. "He made me put it in his mailbox."

There were police staked out at his house. None of them had spotted Damien. The cell phone should still be there. This was getting better and better.

The cell phone would back up Zhara's story. It would also prove that Damien was blackmailing her. "Thank you. If you'll wait here for a moment, I've got a technical expert coming in who is going to help us not only get that collar off of you but put it to use helping us track down Mr. McKnight."

Her eyes connected with his for the first time and she gave a small, brief smile. "Thank you. I just want this nightmare to end."

He wanted to reassure her that it would be ending that day, but he'd spent too many years watching criminals elude justice to do that. The case looked solid, but he knew that things could fall apart in an instant. He'd seen it happen.

He left the interrogation room and headed down the hall towards dispatch. "Do me a favor would you, Kelly?"

The woman behind the desk looked up and smiled. "Sure thing, Henderson. What can I do for you?"

He returned the smile. "Let the team staking out 9113 Sloan Street that they need to check the mailbox for a cell phone. If they find it, I need them to grab it and hang on to it until I can get someone out there to claim it. Would you do that for me?"

She pushed a button on the control panel. "Car 97, this is dispatch. The main office requests that you check the mail box of the residence for a cell phone. Let me know if you find it. If you do, hold onto it until we can send someone to retrieve it. Is that clear?"

She gave Tony a thumbs up to let him know they had received the instructions and would do it. He nodded and headed back down the hallway toward Lindsey's office.

~ ~

"Lindsey, you available to help me with something?" Lindsey Cox looked up from the computer and pushed the glasses back up her nose. She smiled warmly when she saw the face of her visitor.

"What can I do for you?" Tony leaned against the door jam and explained the situation to her.

"So, what do you think? Can you help me?"

Lindsey grabbed a few pieces of equipment from her workspace, hopped off the stool, and headed for the door. "Show me the way, and I'll be happy to do what I can."

Lindsey entered the interrogation room with Tony trailing behind her. The young woman had been up pacing, but took a seat as soon as they entered the room. Tony took a moment to introduce them and Lindsey got to work. She pulled out a small rectangular black box and set it on the table.

She switched it on and dialed a few knobs before she turned to the young lady.

"That should block your friend from being able to send or receive signals from the device around you neck. The next step is to get the collar off of you. I apologize in advance for this, but I'm going to need to get up close and personal if I'm going to be able to figure out where the catch is and how to break it."

She leaned in to examine the collar more closely as her fingers worked their way around, trying to feel where the hinges were. She found a thin seam in the back and rotated the collar so that it, and not the gem, was facing her.

She reached over for a tiny screwdriver, a pair of pliers, and a pair of wire cutters. "I need you to sit very still for me. I don't want to accidentally cut the wrong thing. Can you do that for me?"

Zhara nodded. It took a little tinkering and about 15 minutes of work before Lindsey triumphantly removed the collar from around Zhara's neck. She looked over at Tony. "I'll just take this back to the lab with me and see what we can do about tracking down the source of the signal."

He smiled at her and gave her a thumbs up. She could hear him talking to Zhara as she walked out the door. "You're free to go, Ms. Walinski. I'll follow up with you as soon as I have any more information to give you. In the meanwhile, I strongly recommend that you don't return to your apartment. Do you have somewhere safe to go?"

~ ~

Damien slipped out of bed and headed toward Rita's barn. He wanted to check on Zhara. His pulse raced as he thought about everything he wanted to do to her now that she was truly his. It frustrated him that he had to hide from the police, that he couldn't get her away and just have her to himself, but he could be patient.

He could wait. As long as he could just check on her from time to time, reassure himself she was still there and still under his control, he could manage. Rita was a nice diversion, but she was no substitute for Zhara.

He'd just gotten to the barn and was pulling up the app on his phone when he heard a noise behind him. He turned to look and saw that it was Luke. He slid his phone back in his pocket and crouched down so that he was eye-level with Luke. "Your momma know you're out here?"

Luke's eyes widened and he shook his head.

Damien chuckled and reached out to tussle the boy's hair. "Well, I won't tell if you won't."

Luke grinned and stepped out of the shadows, closer to Damien. "Are you going to be staying with us?"

Damien nodded and smiled at the little boy. He reminded Damien of himself when he was that age. "I sure am."

Luke wrapped his arms around Damien. "I'm glad."

Damien wrapped his arms around Luke and returned the hug. "Me, too, buddy. Me, too."

He stood up and held a hand out for Luke. "What's say we head back to the house and find us something to eat. Your momma's going to be awake soon and I don't want her worrying about where you are when she finds out you're not in bed."

They snuck back inside as quiet as they could be and Damien led Luke into the kitchen. He opened the refrigerator door and pulled out some of the things they'd need for making breakfast. That was one thing he'd learned from his father. He knew how to cook for himself.

He was relieved they'd made it back indoors before Rita could find them. The last thing he wanted was for her to figure out what he'd been up to. He didn't need her asking any questions that he didn't want to answer.

He was nearly finished cooking up the eggs, ham, and fried potatoes when Rita finally wandered in and took a seat at the table. "This must be my lucky day! Two handsome men AND a cooked breakfast."

Luke giggled. "Damien's going to stay with us, Momma. He said so."

She smiled and reached over to tuck an errant strand of hair back in place. "Yes, he's going to stay with us for a bit. Damien, I'm heading into town to pick up a few things. Would you mind staying here and watching out for Luke?"

Damien served a plat to Luke and then one to Rita. "I don't mind. I think Luke and I can make it just fine on our own. Would you mind doing me a favor while you're in town? A friend of mine put a cell phone in my mailbox and I haven't had a chance to go by my house to pick it up since then. I'm worried it's going to get stolen."

Rita finished with the bite she'd just taken. "I can swing by before heading back home and get it for you."

Damien brought his own plate over to the table and set it down. He leaned over and gave Rita a kiss before taking his seat. "Thanks. I appreciate it."

Chapter 24

Officer Robert Clarks watched as a beat up pickup truck pulled up to the mailbox in front of 9113 Sloan Street, opened it, and seemed to be searching for something. Zhara's cell phone lay on the seat beside them. The officer assigned to return it to the police station was on his way, but hadn't gotten there yet.

Robert stepped out of the car and made his way to the passenger side door of the pickup truck. He tapped on the window with her baton. The driver was probably in her late 30's or early 40's, Caucasian, with blonde hair swept up into a ponytail.

She seemed surprised to see the officer and quickly rolled down the passenger side window. "Can I help you, Officer?"

Robert nodded toward the mail box. "Do you live at this house, ma'm?"

She shook her head. "No, sir. My friend does, though. He asked me to retrieve a cell phone that was left for him in the mailbox."

Robert nodded and hooked his thumbs in his belt loops as he rocked back on his heels. "This friend of yours have a name?"

The woman looked concerned. "His name is Damien. Damien McKnight. He is the resident of this place. I promise you, Officer, I'm no thief. You can call and ask him."

Robert continued to ask questions. "I will, but first I need to know a few things. Do you happen to know where Damien McKnight is?"

Her eyes widened and her eyebrows raised. "I do. Is he in some kind of trouble?"

Robert didn't want to give her too much information, just in case she was in on this with him. "I just need you to answer the question, ma'm. Do you know where he is?"

She nodded. "Yes. He's at my place. He called last night and asked if he could stay with me for a while. What's going on?"

Robert frowned. "I need you to come into the station with me, ma'm. I need you to answer some questions. Please step out of the vehicle.'

Her face lost its color. "Please. I can't. I need to get home. My son is with him."

Robert felt his heart stop. "How old is your son, ma'm?"

He could see tears forming in her eyes. "He's just six. Please, is he in danger?"

Robert had a son of his own about that age. He could only imagine how worried she must be. As tempted as he was to order a patrol car to be sent immediately, he had no idea how Damien would react. The last thing the police department wanted or needed was a hostage situation, or for a child to end up dead.

"I can't say for sure, ma'm. That's why I need you to come with me to the station. I need you to tell me everything you know about the man so we can make sure that any plan we create keeps your son safe and you out of harm's way."

~ ~

Zhara collapsed on the couch in the front living room. It felt strange to be back in Gabby and Mike's apartment, but that was the safest place for her right then. It left her accessible to the police and yet out of the reach of Damien.

She flipped on the television, not really caring what was on, just wanting to hear the noise of another human being around her. She didn't want to be alone right at that moment. She rubbed the area around her neck where the collar had been. As grateful as she was to have it off, it felt strange for it not to be there. She'd gotten used to it.

Although cable offered her 294 options, she didn't find anything worth watching on the television and turned it off in disgust. She stood up and paced. She hated waiting. She'd been doing so much of it lately. She wanted to take some kind of action, but she didn't know what action to take. What was there for her to do?

The police were tracking Damien. There was literally nothing to do but wait for Gabby and Mike to get back home before she could catch them up to date on everything that was happening. She wasn't tired enough to sleep yet, though she should be.

She just didn't know what to do with herself. There was no place to channel all of her energy. She wanted to get on her bike and just drive, but the police had asked her to stay in town in case they needed her help or to ask her more questions.

When had her life become centered around Damien? Even with the collar off and the police on the job, she still wasn't free of him. She still couldn't go anywhere she wanted or do anything she wanted because of him. And she would always bear his mark on her skin. That was never going away. It was literally seared into her.

That thought made her angrier than anything else. She wanted to throw something. She wanted to scream at him. But none of those things would change the reality. None of those things would give her back the life she'd had before Damien ruined everything.

"What a mess. What a freakin's mess." She buried her head in her hands. The worst part was knowing that it was her own damn fault.

If she hadn't ignored her sister and brother, if she'd have just listened to their warnings to her about Damien, she wouldn't be in this mess now. But she hadn't believed them. She hadn't wanted to believe them.

~ ~

"He's not like that, Gabby. He loves me!"

Gabby pursed her lips and looked at her younger sister, shaking her head. "He doesn't love you. He's USING you!"

Zhara's face turned red and her eyes narrowed dangerously. "You're just jealous because he loves me and nobody loves you!"

Gabby's face went white. She felt like she'd been slapped in the face. It took every ounce of her self-control not to respond to Zhara in kind.

She lowered her voice and looked her little sister in the face. "You have a lot to learn about love, little sister. I'm just trying to make sure that you don't have to learn it the hard way. But if you insist on chasing after Damien, in spite of everything he's done to you, I can't stop you."

Zhara's jaw clenched and she crossed her arms over her chest. "You're damn right you can't. I'm 18 years old. I can do whatever I please."

Gabby gritted her teeth. "You're right. You're 18 years old. You can do whatever you please, but you cannot and will not do it in this house! Do you understand me?"

Zhara shrugged non-chalantly. "Fine. I'll move in with Damien. He lets me do whatever I want. He says I'm grown and I can make my own choices."

Gabby shook her head. "I'll just bet he does. I don't know what's gotten into you, Zhara, but if Grandpa were still alive you KNOW you would not be acting like this."

Zhara's face went an even darker shade of red. "Don't you dare bring Grandpa into this! You weren't here for him when he died and you weren't here for me! You were too busy worrying about your degree and your friends to be part of my life, so don't think you can come waltzing back into it and start giving me orders. You may be my sister, but you're not my mother!"

Gabby took a deep breath. She felt like she'd been sucker punched in the gut. Tears formed at the corner of her eyes. "Grandpa wanted me to go to school. You know that. I didn't abandon him and I didn't abandon you! I came home every weekend so I could spend time with you. You have no idea what I sacrificed to be part of your life."

Zhara rolled her eyes. Gabby resisted the urge to slap her.

"You came home SOME weekends and even when you were here, you weren't here. You were too busy with your studies or your boyfriend or your friends from college to notice me."

Gabby crossed her arms over her chest and tensed. "I was busy trying to earn a degree so we could have a better life. I apologize for daring to have friends. I'm sorry that I didn't make you the center of my life. I guess I should apologize for not making everything about you!"

Zhara shook her head and slammed her bedroom door behind her. Gabby could hear things being tossed around inside and leaned against the doorjam.

Zhara's voice screamed from inside. "You don't get it. You never got it. You were all I had, and you were gone. You both left me. You and Mike BOTH LEFT ME!"

Gabby sighed and rested her head against the wall. "I did my best to be there for you. So did Mike. I'm sorry it wasn't enough. Is that what this is all about? Is that why you're with Damien? To get back at us?"

Zhara's bitter laughter drifted through the door. "I'm not with him to get back at you. I'm with Damien because while you two were doing your best, he was doing what you weren't. He was there for me when you couldn't bother to be."

Gabby sighed and muttered a question beneath her breath. "But was he really?"

Chapter 25

"Let's start from the top, Ms. Summers. Please tell me everything you can."

Rita looked at the detective. "Damien called me at about 11 pm and asked if I was lonely. He asked if I wanted company for a while. I told him I did. He slept at my place last night. I woke up this morning and he was fixing breakfast. I told him I was planning to go into town. He asked if I would mind picking up a cell phone out of his mail box. I told him I didn't mind. I asked if he would mind looking after Luke, my son, while I was in town. He said he could do that for me. That's all I know. Please, detective, I have to get back home to Luke. I need to make sure he's okay."

The detective didn't change expressions and he didn't respond to her request. "Do you happen to have guns at your house?"

Rita felt her stomach drop. "Of course I have guns, detective. I live on a ranch. There are wild animals that come onto my property quite often in search of food."

The detective made a note on his pad. "Does Mr. McKnight know where those guns are located?"

Rita thought about it. She couldn't recall showing Damien where the guns were. "I don't think so, detective, but I imagine it wouldn't be hard for him to find them. Please, let me go to my son!"

The detective leaned forward. "I will be happy to let you go home when I think it is safe for you to do so. Right now, I am trying to assess the threat level that we might be facing and the best way to approach it so that we don't put your son in an even more dangerous position. Do you understand?"

Rita clenched her jaw and nodded. She felt sick at her stomach. Luke was in danger and it was all her fault. How could she have been so naïve?

The detective sat back in his seat and began to outline a plan. "With everything we know about Mr. McKnight, and everything you've told us, I think the best plan right now is for you to return to the ranch. Please try to act normally. If he asks you what has taken so long, just tell him that you ran into some friends and got caught up in a conversation and lost track of the time. It's the closest thing to the truth you can offer him."

He looked to her to be sure she understood and she nodded. He continued. "We'll give you the cell phone that he wanted you to bring him. Our technician has already transferred the data we needed off of it. "

She waited for him to finish. "Get Luke away from McKnight as quickly as possible, and get yourself and Luke get as far away from the house as you can. An unmarked vehicle will follow you from the station and will wait about an hour before they come in to claim Mr. McKnight. Is that clear?"

Rita nodded.

"Ms. Summers, your life and your son's life may very well depend on you doing exactly what I've asked you to do. Here's the cell phone. We'll be following closely behind you."

The detective passed her the cell phone. "Remember: We'll be right behind you. You have one hour."

~ ~

"Zhara, why didn't you tell me, tell us, what was going on? Why did I have to find this out from the police?" Zhara sat at the table, jaw clenched, her face set in stone. Mike and Gabby sat across from her.

"I was TRYING to protect you."

Gabby raised an eyebrow. "Yeah? And how well did that work out for you?"

Zhara crossed her arms over her chest.

Mike broke in, his voice filled with tension. "You can't keep going off and trying to fix everything on your own. You're not alone. You have us. You need to let us help you!"

She looked from Mike to Gabby and shook her head. "You guys don't get it. I AM alone. You guys have your own thing. You have Purgatory. You have each other. I have NOTHING and I have NO-BODY! I don't even have Damien anymore. Everything is gone. Everything."

Gabby's face flushed red. "How can you sit there and say that? You have US! We're here for you and we always have been!"

Zhara shook her head and glared at Gabby. "No, you haven't been. I know you've tried to be. I get that, but that doesn't change the reality that you left me. You both did. You left me for the military, Mike, and you left me for college, Gabby. You both left me. All I had was Grandpa, but he spent his days sleeping and his nights working the bar. When he was home all we did was fight. He didn't like my friends and he didn't like the way I dressed and he just didn't seem to like anything I did."

Zhara stopped, closed her eyes, and swallowed. "Nothing I did made him happy anymore. And then coming home that day, finding him at the kitchen table like that, like he was still reading his paper."

Tears shimmered in her eyes. "I didn't want to believe he was dead. We fought that morning at breakfast. I wanted to tell him I was sorry. I wanted him to wake up. I wanted it to all be some really bad dream, but it wasn't. And I was alone. Again."

She glared at the two of them. "You have no idea what that was like. None. So don't tell me about how I have you guys. I have you until you find something better. I have you until you decide that you need something else. I am alone!"

Gabby pushed herself away from the table and stood up, putting her hands on the table and leaning into Zhara. "You think you're the only person in the world whose been hurt or lost someone? Really? We've lost people, too. We've lost our mother and our father and our grandfather. We've done everything we can do for you! How much more do we have to do before you realize that in our eyes you are FAMILY??!! "

Her voice shook and tears formed in the corner of her eyes. "We didn't leave you. We went to make a way for you. We went to make sure that we could make your life better. I'm sorry if that meant we had to spend time apart, but we both did everything we could to be there for you as much as we could be."

Zhara looked at her, tears trickling down her face. She shook her head. "But you weren't here! I needed you and you weren't here."

Mike reached out and put a hand on Zhara's arm. "But we are here now. Maybe we weren't then, but we are now. We can be, anyway, if you'll let us be. We can't be there for you, though, if you keep pushing us away. We need you to let us in and let us be part of your life."

Zhara put a hand up to her face and rubbed her eyes. "I want to but I don't know how. Every time I let people in, every time I start counting on them to be there for me, they end up leaving me and my world falls to pieces. It's better if I count on myself. That way, at least the only person who gets let down if I fail is me!"

Mike sighed and put a hand under her chin, gently lifting it so she was looking at him. "Zhara, I learned this in the military. If you keep walking into battles without your buddies to back you up, you're going to keep losing. Yes, buddies get reassigned and sometimes they get wounded and sometimes they die."

He held her gaze. "But you're still better off with your buddies than you are without them. If you lose a buddy, you don't give up on having a buddy. You search out another group of buddies and you add to the number of buddies. We're your buddies. We may get reassigned. We may get wounded. We may die. But as long as we're around, we're still better off together than any of us is alone."

He lowered his voice. "Let us in. We may not have all the answers. We can't solve all the problems. We won't win every battle. But we're much better off fighting the battle together than we are wandering off by ourselves."

He pulled Zhara into his arms and held her tight. She broke down into sobs and buried her face in his chest.

"We love you, Zhara. We will always love you. And to the best of our ability, we will be there for you."

Zhara could feel Gabby's hands stroking her hair and knew she'd been forgiven.

Gabby's voice was soft and tender. "If I didn't love you so much, I wouldn't be so upset with you. How am I supposed to keep you safe when I don't know what's happening? How am I supposed to protect you when you keep going off on your own?"

Zhara shook her head. "You can't. You can't keep me safe. You can't protect me. Nobody can."

Gabby's hands stilled. "I know. You're right. But that doesn't mean I don't want to. That doesn't mean I'm not going to do everything I can to try. Just like you'd do anything you could to protect us."

Zhara's eyes were bloodshot and red-rimmed as she looked up at Gabby. Her voice was hoarse. "I'm sorry. I did try. I just wasn't strong enough. I wasn't good enough to stop him."

Gabby shook her head. "Sweetheart, what happened was not your fault. You did everything you could. Your only mistake was in trying to do it alone."

Chapter 26

"You finished eating, buddy?" Damien couldn't wait to get Luke settled and focused elsewhere so he could check on Zhara. He'd left her alone too long as it was.

Luke swallowed the last bite of his bacon and nodded. "Uncle Damien, do you want to play a game with me?"

No, Damien did not want to play a game with him. He wanted to check on Zhara. But he didn't want to risk Luke figuring out what he was doing or asking too many questions. "How about we watch some TV instead?"

Luke shrugged. "We don't get many channels. Mom doesn't like TV. She says it's bad for my brain."

Damien struggled to keep the frustration out of his voice. "That's too bad, buddy. What kind of games do you have?"

Luke's face brightened and he took Damien by the hand. He led him into the living room and pulled out a selection of board games. Damien resigned himself to spending the morning playing games with the kid. He just hoped Rita would hurry back home.

"You can pick. These are the ones that Mom says are okay for me to play."

Damien noticed a deck of playing cards in the mix and a tall jug of change by the fireplace. He plucked the deck of cards out. "Do you know how to play poker, buddy?

Luke looked up at him and shook his head. Damien grinned. "How about I teach you?"

Luke hesitated. "I don't know if Mom would like that."

Damien shrugged and set the deck of cards back down. "Well, I guess it might be too hard for a little boy like you. I can understand."

Luke's chest puffed out and a scowl crept across his face. "I'm not a little boy. Mom says I'm her little man. I can learn!"

Damien led Luke back into the kitchen and cleaned off the table. "I just bet you can. Go get your mom's jug of change and I'll show you how this game works."

Luke's eyes furrowed together and he bit his lip, but ran into the living room to get the jug. Damien looked around kitchen. How was Damien going to get the kid settled so he could check on Zhara?

His eyes lighted on the liquor cabinet. He knew exactly where Rita kept the key. A little bit of juice, a little bit of alcohol, and Luke would be out in no time.

There was part of him that knew kids Luke's age shouldn't be given alcohol. However, his old man had given it to him and it hadn't done him any harm, so he figured it wouldn't do the kid any harm either.

He reached up above the liquor cabinet for the key. He grabbed it and pulled out a bottle of brandy. The taste was sweet as long as you didn't have too much of it, and mixed well with fruit beverages like the orange juice Rita kept in the fridge.

He grabbed two whiskey glasses from the shelf above the cabinet and covered the bottom of one of the glasses with brandy before pouring orange juice on top. He just finished putting the bottle back when Luke returned dragging his mom's coin jug with him.

~ ~

Rita sped along the road toward her house. She felt chills thinking about what that detective had told her Damien had done. It couldn't be true. It just couldn't.

Guilt for having let him come near her son washed over her. Had she allowed her loneliness and her desire to feel good about herself blind her to the danger? She wouldn't be able to forgive herself if something happened to Luke because of her.

Tears began to form in her eyes as she imagined the worst. She forced herself to stop thinking like that. She wouldn't be able to act normally and get Luke to a safe distance from Damien if she was crying and boo-hooing the whole way. She needed to pull herself together. For Luke's sake.

The stern talking to didn't help quell the rising tide of panic she felt, though. The tears came whether she wanted them to or not. She would just have to claim allergies. She pulled the truck over, gave into the tears for a moment, and let all the fear, the anxiety, the guilt, and the shame wash over her.

A part of her mind woke up and roared, "We don't have TIME for this!"

As if a switch had been flipped inside her, anger came to her rescue, scorching the tears away and giving her the courage to do whatever needed to be done. How dare that man come to her as if he cared and put her son in this kind of danger.

She would be damned if he would hurt one hair on her son's head. And God help him if he already had because that was the only person who would be able to stop her.

She pulled into the long driveway, shut the truck off, and took a moment to calm herself. She forced a smile on her face and grabbed up the cell phone.

She walked into the kitchen to find Damien at the table, staring at his cell phone. He jumped when he hear the door shut and hit the button to switch it off. She pretended not to notice. "Where's Luke?"

Damien smiled up at her. "Taking a little nap. I think his early morning adventures finally caught up with him."

Her heart pounded in her chest. Luke hadn't taken naps since he was two. He didn't take naps unless he was sick. Something was wrong.

However, she didn't let the smile slip from her face. Let him think everything is still okay. "I'll just go check on him."

She headed to Luke's room. The boy was sleeping like an angel. She couldn't help but smile as her heart jumped for joy to see him there. She bent over to give him a kiss and frowned. His breath smelled like alcohol.

The anger she'd worked to suppress ignited into full blown rage. She'd trusted that man with her most precious gem and he'd betrayed that trust. She wasn't going to wait around for the police to show up and escort him off her property. He was going to be leaving her house NOW.

She turned on her heel and marched back into the kitchen. "You gave my son alcohol."

Damien shook his head. "I did not. Luke got into it. I got it away from him and cleaned it all up for you."

He gave her a look as if he were wounded. "You really should do a better job of keeping the alcohol locked up. He really could have hurt himself."

Her eyes narrowed dangerously. "Really? Why didn't you call me and let me know?"

Damien held her gaze and shrugged. "It didn't seem like that big a deal to me. I could tell he hadn't had enough to hurt him and besides, he begged me not to."

Rita's shoulders stiffened. "That was NOT YOUR CALL to make! You should have called me and let me know. You need to leave this house. Now."

Damien stood up and put his hands up. "Rita, honey, calm down. It's not that big a deal."

Every word that Damien said just enraged her further. It was clear he didn't take her feelings, or her trust, seriously. "Get your stuff and GET OUT NOW!"

Damien's face darkened but then he shrugged, grabbed his cell phone and his jacket, and walked out the door. "I don't need this bullshit. It's not my fault you can't take care of your kid."

Rita locked the door behind him and watched him walk toward his motorcycle from the window. She hoped the detective would forgive her for not keeping him there.

~ ~

Tony pulled out of the station ten minutes after Rita. He'd told her he'd give her an hour, but he wanted to be prepared and in place in case something went wrong.

Experience told him that things never went according to plan. Especially when you were dealing with someone as volatile as Damien.

Rita's ranch was halfway between two towns, so he radioed ahead to ask for backup in case Damien got out ahead of him and headed the other direction on the road. He wanted to be sure that he didn't give Damien any chance to escape this time.

He got to the ranch and pulled into the driveway just in time to watch Damien stalking out of the house. Judging by the look on his face, he was not happy about leaving.

Tony swore. At least the boy was safe. He had to stop Damien before he got to his motorcycle or it would be a lot harder to make sure he didn't get away. He floored his vehicle down the driveway. Damien looked up, startled, before taking off running toward the back field.

Tony gunned the vehicle and sped after Damien, hoping to catch him before he could slip into the corn fields. It was near harvest time and it would be nearly impossible to spot him from the ground if he got in there. This was not at all the way he'd hoped things would go.

He stopped his car, got out, and was pulling his gun out of his holster just as Damien reached the edge of the fields.

"Stay right where you are, Mr. McKnight, turn around slowly, and put your hands in the air. I will shoot if necessary, but I'd rather not have to do that."

Damien turned around to face him and put his hands in the air. Tony aimed the gun at Damien, just in case Damien got the idea to run.

"Walk slowly toward me and keep your hands in the air." Tony watched as Damien slowly walked toward the car. He kept his gun trained on Damien the whole way. Frightened men often did incredibly stupid things and Damien had good reason to be afraid of the law right now.

He breathed a sigh of relief when he finally got Damien cuffed and placed into the back of his squad car. Things were far from over, but at least Damien was under control for the time being.

Chapter 27

"Mr. McKnight, do you understand why you're here?" Tony sat down in front of Damien to question him, placing Damien's case file to his right. Damien's eyes were almost a pitch black in color and his jaw was clenched. His arms were crossed over his chest.

Tony knew what that meant. Damien believed Tony was the enemy and that meant he would have trouble getting anything out of him until Damien was convinced that Tony was on his side...or at least could be persuaded to be. Damien stared at Tony in mute silence.

Tony opened up the file and spent a little time pretending to examine the papers in front of him. "You have been accused of some very serious charges, Mr. McKnight. Kidnapping. Extortion. Aggravated assault. Blackmail. Fleeing a police officer."

He looked up. "Blackmail, on its own, carries a potential of 10 years in prison. Aggravated assault, another 10 years. Kidnapping – goodness, you don't even want to know. Now, I would very much like to help you. I would like to understand your side of the story. I am sure that not everything that's been said about you or about what happened here is entirely accurate, but I'm going to need you to cooperate with me in order to do that."

Damien stared up at the ceiling, still mute. "If you don't talk, then I'm afraid that the only testimony that will be put forth is the testimony of those who are speaking against you. Don't you want a fair chance to clear your name? Or shall I assume that you are guilty?"

Damien's face reddened a bit. His gaze returned to Tony and he shrugged. "You're just like the rest. You're going to assume I'm guilty anyway. I don't stand a chance. Why should I talk?"

Tony nodded. "You might be right. I might be just like the rest. Then again, I might be somebody who is willing to give you the benefit of the doubt. When I was growing up, I had this cousin. She was always starting stuff with me. She would throw things at me, destroy my toys, call me names. She never got in trouble for any of that."

He paused to assess the impact of the story on Damien. Those black eyes were focused on him. He continued the story. "But anytime I tried to handle it myself, any time I did something back, she would go running to my aunt and complain about how mean I was to her. I know a lot about people being falsely accused, or at the very least there being more to the story than there appears at first glance. That's why I became a detective. I wanted to make sure we got to the truth – the whole truth."

Damien shifted in his seat and his shoulders relaxed just slightly. Tony knew that was a good sign. Damien was listening, even if he wasn't quite ready to open up yet. He needed something to get Damien talking, something that would be safe for him. "How long have you known Zhara Walinski?"

Damien rocked back in his chair a moment and then tipped the front feet back down. "I don't know. About six years, I guess."

Tony wrote down a note. That confirmed at least part of Zhara's story.

"How did the two of you meet? I mean you were – what? 22? She was about 16?"

Damien shrugged again and looked away for a moment before looking back at Tony. "Yeah. That's probably about right. It was a graduation party for one of my old football buddies. Zhara was there with Gabby and Mike. I didn't know she was 16 until later. She sure looked grown up to me."

Tony made another note. That coincided with things he'd been told by Gabby and Zhara. "How would you characterize your relationship with Ms. Walinski?"

Damien scowled for a moment and the tension reappeared in his shoulders. His jaw clenched again. Tony made a mental note.

Zhara was definitely an emotional trigger for Damien. That was the leverage he needed to get the man to open up. All he needed to do was figure out the dynamics of their relationship and he could get Damien talking.

"Bitch is crazy. She doesn't know what she wants. One minute she's all over me and the next minute she hates me and doesn't want anything to do with me."

Damien shrugged. "I can't make her happy no matter what I do."

There was an edge to Damien's voice that Tony recognized. Tony pulled a picture of the collar from out of the envelope and pushed it in front of Damien. "Is that why you made her put on the collar?"

Damien snorted. "I didn't make her. She chose to do it. I never forced Zhara to do anything. If that bitch told you otherwise, she's lying."

Tony slid forward Zhara's cell phone. "Did you tell Zhara that if she didn't put on the collar that you would put this and other photographs all over the internet?"

Damien's face darkened. His eyes snapped to Tony's face. "Where'd you get that?"

Tony shook his head. "That's not the right question. Where I got it doesn't matter. What does matter is what's on it. Can you explain the text message stating, "There's plenty more where this one came from. Betray me and I'll make her famous. Play time's not over yet" and the accompanying image?"

Damien growled. "You took that out of my mail box. You had no right to do that!"

Tony held Damien's gaze. "Doesn't this phone belong to Ms. Walinski?"

Damien's scowl deepend. "And?"

Tony tapped the phone. "Why would you think it was in your mailbox, then, Damien?"

Damien seemed to recognize that he'd made a mistake. His face slid back into the mask he'd worn earlier. "I want a lawyer. I got a right to a lawyer."

Tony groaned internally. Once the lawyer got here, it was going to be a lot harder to get unfiltered information from Damien. "You do have the right to a lawyer, and I'll be happy to get one for you, but you're going to find that I'm a lot less sympathetic once the lawyer gets here. I am the best hope you have of walking out of here without spending a decade or more in federal prison. Let me help you, Damien. Talk to me."

Damien's jaw remained clenched. "I want a lawyer. I'm not talking until I get one."

~ ~

"Ladies, pack your bags. We are heading out for a weekend in Reno. " Gabby and Zhara looked at one another and then back at Mike. The bewilderment on their face was evident.

Zhara was the first to speak. "Reno? Why? What's the occasion?"

Mike grinned. "No occasion, Miss Thing. Just a time for family bonding and a chance to forget our problems for a few nights. Who needs more reason than that?"

Gabby frowned briefly. "I don't know, Mike. Who's going to watch the bar while we're gone? Besides, I don't really feel like going anywhere."

Mike kept the smile on his face but he was concerned about Gabby. Ever since the incident with Damien, she'd stopped going out. "I've got Edward and a few of the guys who are taking over for us for the next two days. Things will be fine. You need this, Gabby. I know you don't feel like going anywhere, but do it for us. We need this, and we need you to be there with us. Don't we, Zhara?"

Zhara caught Mike's eyes and nodded. "I have no idea where we're going, but I do agree with the needing to get out. We haven't gone anywhere as a family in months. Come on, Gabby. I'm sure it'll be fun."

Gabby reluctantly agreed. "Fine. I'll go. Just don't expect me to enjoy myself."

Mike sighed. That was probably as good as he was going to get out of her. "Great! Let's load up. I've already got the car packed. We can be there in 2 hours. The concert starts at 8. We'll do a little shopping first and then head over."

Gabby raised an eyebrow as she looked at her brother. "Shopping? What kind of concert is this?"

Mike grinned. "You'll see when we get there"

~ ~

John stepped out onto the stage and his heart skipped a beat as he spotted three familiar faces in the crowd. He quickly calmed himself and took a seat at the grand piano, pouring every ounce of what he felt in that moment into his playing.

He'd honestly never expected to see Zhara again. There was so much he wanted to say to her. So many questions that were running through his mind. He fought against the hope that surged forward, trying not to let himself believe that she might have finally seen past Damien's dubious allure to choose him.

He finished his set, stood, and received the applause from the crowd. He bowed and then headed back stage, hoping to slip out among the crowd and catch the three before they could leave.

He breathed a sigh of relief as he noticed them. "Zhara, Mike, Gabby...to what do I owe this pleasure?"

He greeted the three of them but his eyes betrayed him. They were fastened on Zhara's face as if he were trying to memorize every detail of it. The smile that stretched across her face as he approached ignited the spark of hope into a growing flame.

Mike smiled at him and then looked at Zhara and Gabby. "Just treating the ladies to a well-deserved night out."

There were tears shimmering in Zhara's eyes and John swallowed. Mike and Gabby made their excuses and headed for the bar. John hardly noticed. Fear that Zhara was going to tell him that she wasn't ready to be with him or some other thing rose to the forefront of his mind.

"I'm sorry."

John heard the words coming out of Zhara's mouth but didn't understand them. "For what?"

Zhara closed her eyes and a single tear slid down her cheek. He hesitated before brushing it away. She opened her eyes and looked at him. "For hurting you. For pushing you away. For not telling you why I couldn't talk to you that night. For not trusting you."

He took a step closer. "You're here now. If you're willing to let me in, I meant what I wrote to you that night. I still love you. I will always love you."

Another tear made its way down the other cheek. "I don't know why you do. I don't know that I can return it to you. But I do believe that. I believe you love me. I just don't know how to love you."

John took another step forward and opened his arms wide. "I can teach you, if you'll let me."

Zhara closed the gap and into his embrace. He could feel the tears dampening the front of his shirt as the words spilled out of her. "You'll get tired of me. You'll get tired of me hurting you. I'm broken and I don't have anything to give you but my brokenness. I'll cut you and I won't mean to. The closer you get to me, the more I'm going to hurt you."

John kissed the top of her head. "We are all broken, Zhara. All of us. We all cut one another and we don't mean to. We all hurt each other the closer we get to one another. All we have to give one another is our brokenness. The only difference is that some of us know we are broken and some of us are afraid to admit that we are. "

Zhara buried her face in his chest. "I don't want to give you a broken heart. I want to give you all of my heart, but broken is all I have."

John wrapped his arms tightly around her. "Oh, my love. Don't you understand? Love is what makes us whole. We are all broken until love enters in and finds us. Love is the only glue strong enough to fuse those broken pieces back together again."

He felt Zhara relax in his arms. She lifted her head and looked him in the eyes. "John, you frighten me."

He frowned and started to pull back, but her grip on him was too tight. "Frighten you? How?"

She bit her lip and her brow furrowed. "Because the more I know you, the more I want you in my life and yet the more afraid I am that you're going to leave me, just like all the rest. And I don't think I could handle that. "

John took her hands and lifted them to his lips. "Zhara, we all fear losing those we love. We fear the emptiness we feel when they aren't there. I can't promise you that I will never leave you because death is something that comes for all of us, and I can't control death nor choose the time of my own."

He paused and kissed her hand again. "What I can promise you is that if you turn away from love because you fear the loss of it, you will miss out on the opportunities for love that come your way each day. Love is like the tide. It washes into our life and then washes back out, leaving in its wake a trail of treasures to remember it by. We can enjoy the tide while it is there or we can refuse to wade into it because we know it will soon be gone and miss the joy that might have been ours if only we'd had the courage. The choice is up to us. I have loved and I have lost, and each loss hurt, but the love was worth the cost to gain. I am a better man for the time that love was there."

John looked into Zhara's amber eyes and pulled her closer to him. "What is it to be, my love? Shall we dance while the tide is in or do we stay apart for fear of loss and lose out on the opportunity to dance?"

Zhara reached up to cup his face in her hands and kissed him with a tender passion before letting him go. "Let's dance."

Chapter 28

"Ms. Montrose? This is Detective Henderson. I wanted to let you know that we have Mr. McKnight in custody. I can't tell you more than that at this point, but I wanted to let you know that he has been apprehended."

Gabby had spent the last few weeks waiting to hear those words. She thought they would bring peace and security with them, but neither came. "Thank you, Detective. I appreciate you taking the time to notify me. What happens next? When is the trial?"

Henderson hesitated for a moment. "We are taking his statement right now. Once we have all the information from him, we will present our findings to the judge. It will be up to the judge to determine whether or not we have sufficient evidence to hold him for longer than 72 hours. If we can hold him, the judge will also determine whether he can post bail or not, and how much that bail will be. If he can't post bail, he will likely be in jail until the trial."

Anger that had been simmering beneath the surface rose inside her and would not be denied its exit. She practically screamed into the phone. "IF? If there is enough evidence to hold him? The man fucking KIDNAPPED me and would have RAPED me if I hadn't lied to him to stop him. What do you mean there might not be sufficient evidence?"

Gabby winced as all eyes turned in her direction at the outburst. She felt her cheeks burning and tears of shame sprang to her eyes. Mike put a hand on her shoulder, but she shrugged it off without looking at him, grabbed up her purse and headed away from the crowd. She was looking for a more private place to talk. She found a deserted hallway and paced the length of it as the discussion continued.

"I am sorry, Ms. Montrose. I know how this must –"

Gabby cut him off. She had no time or space for platitudes. "Don't fucking tell me you KNOW how I must feel. You don't. I'm so sick of people telling me they understand and they get it. They don't. Nobody does. You have no idea what it was like. I didn't know if I was going to live or die down there."

She felt sick at her stomach and tears of anger refused to be denied as they spilled down her cheeks. "So don't even begin to pretend you understand for one minute what I went through, okay? And to hear you tell me that there might not be enough evidence to even hold him, let alone get him put away?"

"Ms. Montrose, I am sorry. There's really nothing I can do about the situation. I will let you know if anything further develops. There is a good chance the judge will acknowledge the evidence as valid and Mr. McKnight will find himself in permanent police custody, but I don't want to promise what I can't deliver."

Gabby's world felt like it was turning upside down. How could a man kidnap her and hold her prisoner and nearly rape her and he could still walk free? How was this justice? How was this right?

"Ms. Montrose? Are you still there?"

She couldn't respond. She knew if she spoke a single word she would shatter into pieces. Instead, she just hung up the phone. She sat on a bench in the hallway, staring at the floor, trying to collect herself.

Mike found her and sat down beside her, wrapping her up in a hug. "I won't ask if you're okay. It's obvious you're not. Just know that I'm here for you."

Gabby barely heard him. She allowed him to embrace her, but his warmth wasn't enough to overcome the chill that was overtaking her. She felt like everything she'd counted on and believed to be true about life had been ripped away from her in a single instant and she'd entered this alternate dimension where good guys don't save the day and bad guys walk free. "Fuck. This."

Her head snapped up. "Fuck this whole thing. I'm not waiting around for someone to decide whether Damien is guilty or innocent. I KNOW he's guilty. I know exactly what was done to me and to Zhara. I don't need a judge and I don't need the law. Let them do whatever the fuck it is they do. I'm going to take that bastard down."

~ ~

Mike's lips pursed and his brows drew together until there was a tiny crease between them. "Gabby –"

Gabby cut him off as she stood up. Rage coursed through her veins and she shook with the force of it. "Don't you DARE tell me to be reasonable or to wait on the law. I'm done with living in fear, waiting for that guy or the next to do something to me. I'm DONE WITH THAT! Do you hear me?"

Mike's mouth opened and then it closed abruptly. He stood up and his eyes glittered dangerously. "Is that what you thought I was going to tell you? To be reasonable? To let other people handle it for you?"

Gabby crossed her arms over her chest. "Weren't you?"

He crossed his arms over his own chest and stared at her. "I was going to ask you if he's really worth this. Is he worth the risk of going to jail? Is he worth the risk of us being separated again, maybe for the rest of our lives? I promised Mom and Grandpa both, Gabby, that I would protect you and I failed. I'm sorry. I can't go back into the past and change things. I can't make it all better. I wish I could. But if we do this, we go after him and we take things into our own hands, aren't we letting him destroy us? Is he worth that?"

Gabby lowered herself onto the seat and put her head in her hands. "How? How do I make the nightmares go away? How do I stop his face from intruding into my thoughts? He took everything from me and I just want it back! How is it right that he doesn't have to live like this and I do?"

Mike put an arm around her shoulder. "When I got out of the military, you know I wasn't right. Hell, I'm still not alright. I'm a bar tender in a tiny town. I have no life, no girlfriend. All I have is you and Zhara. But somehow being in the bar, the routine of it, the familiarity of it, that helped. As long as I work in the bar, a piece of Grandpa's still alive. And that feels good to me. It's solid. It's stable. But I still have the nightmares, Gabby.

He leaned his head against hers. "I still see the faces of the people whose lives I took. I didn't have a choice but to take them, but I can't erase those faces from my mind. Maybe I don't even want to. Maybe as long as I can remember those faces and feel guilt for what I did, it reminds me that I'm still human and not the monster part of me believes I am. I don't want to tell you that you are going to be able to make the nightmares go away. I haven't figured out how to do that for myself. But you can live with them. You can learn from them."

Gabby didn't respond, and Mike didn't press her. The silence grew until she spoke. Her voice was so soft he almost didn't catch the words. "At least the ghosts that haunt your dreams can't hurt you anymore. The ghost that haunts mine is still out there. And I don't know how to live with that."

He looked at his hands for a moment, studying them as if he'd just noticed them for the first time. "I don't know what the answers are, but I will promise you that we will look for them together. We will find a way to make sure that Damien can't hurt anybody else the way he's hurt our family. I don't know how, but there has got to be an answer that doesn't involve adding to the ghosts in our collection. Please, trust me?"

Gabby leaned up against him, considering everything he'd said. Anger gave way to determination. "He's taken enough from us. I don't want him to take my freedom or my family away from me. You're right. There's got to be a better way to stop him. I think I know who to talk to. Someone who might be able to give me some answers. I haven't talked to him in years, but I think he'd be willing to help."

Mike gave her a sidelong glance. "Oh? Him? Is this someone I know?"

Gabby shook her head. "Just a guy I knew my freshman year of college. I haven't seen him since then. But I did hear he went on to graduate law school and then came back to Reno and set up practice."

Mike nodded. "Hopefully, he won't charge too much. We make a pretty decent living from the bar, but we're not rich."

The corner of Gabby's mouth turned up in a smrk. "Oh, I don't think that's going to be a problem. He owes me one."

She pulled out her phone and looked at the time. "It's getting late. I think we should extend our hotel stay for an evening and then collect Zhara from the bar. We've got business here in Reno."

Chapter 29

"Wow, Gabby. So good to see you! Come in, come in. It's been far too long. And this gentleman is?"

She stepped into the well-lit office and took her seat in the leather chair parked in front of the polished oak desk where Brian's name-plate rested.

Brian took a seat behind the desk and focused those warm brown eyes of his on her. "Tell me about the case, and let me see what I can do to help you."

It felt so awkward telling him about the abduction and the near rape. There were parts of the story she found herself having to stop and wipe the tears from her eyes as the memories of what happened came back full force. He didn't interrupt her, he just listened. She finally finished and fixed her eyes on him, hoping that he would be able to make sure Damien could never, ever touch her again.

His answer was not reassuring in the least. "You want easy answers, and I understand that, but I'm afraid there aren't any. The legal system doesn't work like that. I wish I could tell you otherwise, but I am not going to lie to you. Damien may be guilty, but without hard evidence, it's unlikely that the District Attorney is going to be able to convict him. They may not even proceed to trial."

These were not the words she wanted to hear. Her eyes filled with tears and her voice choked with suppressed emotion. "But my testimony – our testimony – surely that should be enough, shouldn't it?"

He didn't flinch from her question. His eyes were full of compassion, but his words hit like stones. "Should it? Do you really want a justice system that works that way? Let's pretend that it's you being accused of a crime. Testifying against you is this man and his closest friend. You know you're innocent, but there are two witnesses saying you did it. In your version of the justice system, that would be enough to convict you. Do you see how easily such a system can be manipulated?"

She felt the flush of anger and clenched her fists. "I'm not falsely accusing him! That's not what's happening here."

He held up a hand to stop her. "I'm not saying you're falsely accusing him. I'm saying that protecting people from false accusations is exactly why it requires more than the testimony of two witnesses to convict someone – especially when those witnesses know one another and have good reason to back one another up. You are asking for a conviction on the basis of witness testimony alone. The law needs more than that. It needs evidence that this was not a consensual episode of two women with a man and then those two women changed their minds later."

Gabby's mouth dropped open and she could feel the heat of her anger all the way up her face. "That is NOT what happened! The man nearly raped me."

Brian kept his calm. "I believe you. But I'm not the one you need to convince. I'm not talking about what I believe or don't believe. I'm talking about what it will take to convict this man of the crimes you are saying he committed."

She crossed her arms in front of her chest and looked away while she struggled to regain her composure. "This is unbelievable. I thought you'd be able to help me."

He sighed heavily. "You have no idea how much I wish things were different. I wish it were as easy as you want it to be, but it isn't. I can help you. I just need you to understand what you're up against if you choose to pursue this. The burden of proof is on you. You have to prove he's guilty, and based on what you've told me so far, I don't think you have the evidence to do that."

She felt her hopes die with those words. Tears spilled down her cheeks and she grabbed a tissue from the box on his desk, mercilessly wiping at them. "I can't prove he drugged me. I can't prove he was holding me captive in that God forsaken bunker. I can't prove he forced the alcohol into me. I can't prove he was threatening to rape me, or that I didn't want him to unbutton my blouse or take those pictures of me. I can't prove any of it. He didn't actually rape me, so there's no semen, just the pictures he took while I was passed out, and by your statement, all he has to do is claim I gave him permission while I was drunk and that's enough!"

He held her gaze. "Sexual assault cases are extremely difficult to prove, especially when there are no bodily fluids to collect. I wish there were more I could do to help you, but unless you can turn up physical evidence that proves you were not willing – besides your testimony and that of your sister – this case isn't likely to go in your favor. You'd be wasting your money."

She felt her jaw tremble as she heard the words coming out of his mouth. Everything she'd feared was being confirmed. "So that's it? I'm just supposed to forget about what he did? I don't know how to do that. I can't sleep. I close my eyes and I'm right back in that bunker, scared that I'm going to die, scared that he'll abandon me and I'll die all by myself in that darkness. Even more scared of what he will do if he doesn't. Why does he get to wreck my life and go scott free all because I had the presence of mind to stop him from doing worse to me than he'd already done? Where is justice for me?"

He stood up and walked around to the front of the desk, taking a seat in the chair beside her. He took her hands in his. "Look. I can't help you convict him, but maybe I know someone who can help you with the rest of it. She's a trained victim's advocate. Give her a call. I think she can help you."

She gritted her teeth and yanked her hands away. "I need justice. I don't need an advocate."

He pulled a card out of his card holder, turned it over, and wrote down a woman's name and phone number. He pressed it into Gabby's hand. "Call her. I've seen how these things go. Even if you manage to put Damien away, that's not going to magically fix everything for you. It won't make the nightmares stop. It won't take away the fear you're living with and the panic and anxiety attacks. If you don't get help processing what happened to you, these things are going to keep haunting you."

She stood up, crumpled the business card he'd given her, and dumped it in her purse. She looked down at him. She was trembling with anger. "There's NOTHING wrong with me. Damien's the problem, not me."

He stood up and shook his head. "That's not what I'm saying. I'm not saying something is wrong with you. I'm saying that you're a normal human being who has been through a very traumatic experience. You need help processing things – anyone in your shoes would. That doesn't make you weak. It makes you human."

She turned on her heels and walked out the door. "Thanks for nothing."

She faintly heard his voice on her way out. "You're welcome, Gabs."

It wasn't his fault. He was just telling her how things worked. But it felt like such a complete and utter betrayal of her trust. He was supposed to help her. He was supposed to be able to fix things for her. But when she'd needed him most, he couldn't come through. Nobody could. She was all alone.

~ ~

"Don't you want to eat something first?" Mike raised an eyebrow as Gabby poured herself a generous serving of whiskey and began to drink it. She frowned and rolled her eyes.

"I'm not hungry. And I don't need a nanny."

He chose not to respond to that. "I take it your meeting with the attorney friend didn't go well?"

Gabby shrugged. "He just basically told me the same thing the Detective did. They probably aren't going to have enough evidence to put Damien away. My testimony, Zhara's testimony, it doesn't mean anything. What we went through down there doesn't mean anything. That bastard is most likely going to walk and there's nothing that can be done about it. Nothing."

Mike felt himself getting angry at the whole situation. He understood the need for caution in putting away criminals as much as the next person, but when it came to his sister, those things didn't matter. What mattered to him was that Gabby wasn't okay and neither she nor Zhara were safe.

"If we can't put Damien away, maybe we should be the ones getting away."

Gabby whirled around and faced Mike. Her eyes were round and wide. "What do you mean?"

He hated to say the words, felt almost like he was betraying Grandpa with them, but felt they needed to be said anyway. "I mean what if we sell Purgatory and leave town, go someplace so you never have to deal with Damien again?"

Gabby sat down carefully and stared at Mike. "Leave Purgatory? But Grandpa-"

Mike cut her off. "Grandpa charged me with protecting you and Zhara. I can't do that with Damien around. If selling the bar is what it takes, I'm all for it. But you own half of it. It's your decision, too."

Gabby frowned and stared down into her drink. She took another sip and closed her eyes for a moment. "I don't know. Maybe we think on it for a little bit. It's hard to imagine my life without that bar in it."

Mike stood up and walked over to the window. "I know what you mean. But I also know that, in the end, what matters most to me isn't the bar or the memories that came with it. It's you and Zhara. And maybe we've all been tied to Purgatory for just a little too long. Maybe it's time to finally put the past behind us and get a fresh start."

Gabby nodded a little and then took another sip. "Maybe it is."

Chapter 30

"Did I miss a funeral or something?" Zhara looked at Mike and Gabby, seated side-by-side on one of the hotel beds. The joy she'd felt from her evening with John faded to be replaced by anxiety and fear. Neither of them looked happy. Gabby was clutching her glass tightly.

Mike looked up and gave her a weak smile. "No, we were just discussing Purgatory, that's all."

Zhara's stomach clenched. "What about it?"

Gabby looked up at her and then back down at her drink. She took a sip, as if searching for courage, before she replied to Zhara. "We're talking about selling it."

Zhara felt her knees weaken and sat down on the chair near the bed. "You can't be serious."

Mike sighed and ran a hand across his face. "We can be, and we are. As much as we both hate to let it go, it's time we all move on."

Zhara looked back and forth between the two of them and shook her head. She couldn't quite believe what she was hearing. "But

Grandpa—"

Gabby's mouth turned down suddenly and she looked up. Her eyes glittered with tears. Her voice was thick and her face was pale. "Don't start with that. Grandpa didn't give us Purgatory to keep us held there forever. He gave it to us so we would have something to use to build a better future. Purgatory's done that. It has gotten us this far. But that doesn't mean we have to stay there forever."

Mike put a hand on Gabby's shoulder and looked over at Zhara. "Gabby and I were barely keeping that place going on our own as it is. I can't do it alone, and Gabby's just not up to it anymore."

Zhara's heart sank. "I could help! I helped Grandpa during those four years that you guys were gone. I could do it."

Mike shook his head. "Even if that were true, Zhara, there's still Damien. As long as we hold onto Purgatory, Damien will still be able to make our lives hell. The only way to truly be free of him is to let go of Purgatory."

Zhara felt her eyes filling with tears and fought as hard as she could not to let them fall. "But the police—"

Gabby's eyes narrowed. Her voice was harsh and bitter. "Aren't going to do a damn thing about him. Now, or ever. There's not enough "proof" that he did anything. If I'd have let him rape me, we might have had a case, but the police are telling me it's our word against his and we have no physical evidence that proves this was not a consensual activity. So unless he suddenly grows a conscience or makes a major mistake and accidentally confesses, he's going to be free to continue making our lives a living hell."

Zhara's mouth dropped open and her eyes widened. The realization that nothing was going to happen, that Damien was going to go free in spite of everything, was like a nightmare. "But the pictures, Gabby –"

Gabby's mouth formed a single, thin straight line. "Don't prove anything. They don't prove I didn't give him permission to take those."

Zhara shook her head, trying to dispel the growing sense of dread she felt. "But the messages, the blackmail?"

Gabby sighed and took another drink. "That's the only thing we might be able to get him on, honestly. But I'm not holding my breath. And I need to get away from there, Zhara. Please understand. I can't live in that same town with him. As long as he's there, I will always end up looking over my shoulder, wondering what he's going to do next."

Zhara looked up at the ceiling and struggled for control over her emotions. She felt like she was losing the only family she had left in the world. As if he sensed what she was thinking, Mike reached for her hand. "We're not leaving you behind, Z. You're welcome to come with us, no matter where we go. This could be your chance to start fresh, too, get away from Damien and make a clean break. Reno's not that far from home, and maybe you could go to school. You've got plenty of options."

His words broke through every fear she had. The reassurance that she wasn't going to be left behind or forgotten was exactly what she'd needed. "I can't lose you guys. I can't."

Gabby and Mike were there in a moment, surrounding her and reassuring her of their love, before she could finish the words. She couldn't contain the tears that forced their way through to the surface.

"You're never, ever going to lose us. We are family. That's not going to change. We love you, Z."

Fears that her relationship with Damien and the things that had happened as a result would be enough to finally push them away were released with every choking sob that made its way past her throat. "I'm sorry. I'm so sorry."

Those were the only words she could manage in reply. Her heart ached for everything she'd put them through, for all the worry and the pain and the loss that she'd caused because of her relationship with Damien.

Gabby's arms wrapped tight around her and Gabby's own tears mingled with hers. "I'm sorry, too. I'm sorry I wasn't there for you the way you needed me to be. I'm sorry I couldn't protect you from him. I'm sorry that it took all of this to finally understand what was really happening."

Zhara rested her head on Gabby's shoulders. "It was not your fault. I know that. You tried to be there. I just couldn't see it."

The three of them sat there for a moment, hugging each other close, before breaking apart. They sat silent, close but not quite touching, for a long stretch.

Mike's deep voice was the first to break the silence. "Where do we go from here?"

Gabby looked over at him and then back at Zhara. "I've got a bachelor's degree in social work that's doing me absolutely no good working as a barmaid. This whole thing has made me realize that's the best way to fight against stuff like this – to stop it before it has a chance to begin. I've been thinking about going back to school and getting my master's degree, maybe working as a crisis counselor or something. What about you, Z? If you could do anything, what would you do with your life?"

Zhara frowned and shrugged. "I don't know, honestly. If there's one thing I've realized out of this whole mess is that I spent most of the past six years with Damien at the center of my universe. Everything I did and said and wanted revolved around what he was thinking or doing or felt or wanted. I built my whole identity around him, to the point where I don't know who I am or what I want anymore. I think I just want the space and time to figure that out. What about you, Mike?"

Mike frowned for a moment and then looked over at Zhara. "I've thought about that a lot over these last few weeks. I think I want to apply to the police academy. Maybe I can do some good working for the law that I can't do right now."

Zhara grinned over at Mike. "Just don't expect me to call you Officer Montrose at home, got it?"

He gave her a playful nudge. "Whatever. I still have to actually get selected for the Academy."

They fell silent again, each one lapsing into their own thoughts, until Gabby's voice broke through the quiet. "I guess that's one thing I can thank Damien for."

Zhara and Mike both stared at Gabby. "Thank him? For what?"

Gabby looked at the both of them. "He forced us to deal with the problems we'd been ignoring for years, and he's forcing us to move on with our lives rather than continuing to let the past hold us back. I'm not saying I'm grateful for what he did to me, or to us, but I doubt we'd have gotten to this point if he hadn't done it."

Zhara's mouth opened and then abruptly closed. She took a deep breath. "I guess what my grandpa used to say is true. Sometimes you have to go through Hell to be ready to appreciate the beauty of Heaven."

Mike chuckled. "Well, I don't know if Reno counts as Heaven, but it's bound to be better than the Hell we've just gone through. I'm certainly willing to give it a try."

Gabby nodded. "I am, too. It's going to be tough saying goodbye to Purgatory, but I think I'm ready for it."

Zhara sighed. "I will go wherever you guys go. As much as I hate to lose Purgatory, you guys are home to me. As long as I have the two of you, I can live anywhere."

Gabby gave Zhara a sly grin. "It probably doesn't hurt anything that if you're living in Reno, you'll be closer to a certain piano player."

Zhara blushed and looked at her sister. "Well, no. It doesn't hurt that Reno's where John lives. It'll make it easier to see him. But John and I aren't rushing anything. I'm not sure I'm ready for more than just dating him right now."

Gabby smiled and patted Zhara's leg. "It's good that you're taking your time. John does seem to be a better fit for you than Damien ever was, but there's no harm in giving yourselves time to get to know one another."

Zhara looked over at her brother and sister. "What about the two of you? When are you guys going to get out there and find someone?"

Gabby looked down at her hand for a minute. "After I left college, after my engagement ended, things just happened so fast. There was just never any time, really, between taking care of Purgatory and watching over you."

Mike shrugged. "I'm open to it, I just haven't found anyone that interests me."

Gabby nodded. "Small towns make for a really small dating pool. And as long as we had Purgatory, well, moving wasn't an option. I'm not sure I'm really up for dating right now but being in Reno would make meeting someone a whole lot easier."

Mike stood up and stretched. "So it's decided then? We're selling off Purgatory and buying a place here in Reno?"

Zhara looked at Gabby. Gabby didn't hesitate. "It's decided. It's high time we leave Purgatory behind and Reno's as good a place as any to go. I even know a few people who might be able to help us find a place and get settled in. Of course, we'll have to wait until Purgatory sells, which might take some time."

Mike shook his head. "It won't take as long as you think. Some of my buddies asked me about buying it from us a while back, but I wasn't ready to sell then. If they're still interested, we could be out of there by spring."

Zhara's eyes widened and she looked over at Mike. "Wow. That soon, huh? It's hard to imagine."

Gabby looked hopeful. "Do you think we could be gone that soon? As much as I'll miss our place, I can't wait to put that whole thing behind us."

Mike shrugged. "It's no guarantee, but I do think there's a good chance they'll still be interested. What do you say we go take a drive around town and get a feel for the neighborhoods while we're here?"

Zhara stood up and reached for her phone. "I think that sounds like a great idea. Maybe John would know some good places to start looking. I'll text him and ask."

As much as she didn't really want to leave Purgatory behind, she was starting to warm up to the idea of being closer to John. Maybe this was exactly what everybody needed. A fresh start and a fresh chance to get over the things that were hurting them. That was something Zhara knew she needed.

Chapter 31

"My client has done nothing wrong."

Tony stared at Camille Sanders, the lawyer Damien hired, and silently wished he could slap that smug expression off her perfectly made up face. Instead he looked down at the case file and began reading off the list of charges against Damien.

"Kidnapping. Sexual assault. Extortion. Resisting arrest. Providing alcohol to a minor." He closed the case file and crossed his arms. "Shall I continue?"

She shrugged and held his gaze. "You can continue all you like, it won't change the facts. My client was acting in good faith on a request the two women in question made that he help them act out their sexual fantasies. He is the victim of these two women's malicious attempt to smear his good name."

Every instinct that Tony had developed over years of working cases told him that what the lawyer just stated was a lie, but even he had to admit that it was just plausible enough an explanation for the events that a judge might well dismiss the case based on that alone.

His gut tightened. The last thing he wanted to do was let this dirtbag back out there to hurt more women, but the law was the law. If he couldn't get Damien to confess, there was not going to be a case. "Let's say you're right and Damien's the real victim here. That doesn't explain the fact that he resisted arrest. It doesn't explain his providing alcohol to a minor."

Camille leaned forward and a smile stretched across her ruby lips. He could smell the faintest hint of her perfume and recognized it as a new fragrance called Nightshade. It seemed appropriate for a woman like her. "Resisting an unlawful arrest isn't against the law. Since my client did nothing wrong, you had no right to arrest him in the first place. He was understandably confused and frightened when you came after him. I think a jury will understand that, don't you?"

This case was slipping away from him far too quickly. He clutched at the one thing that might be able to get Damien. "Alright. Let's say that's the case. What about the charge of providing alcohol to a minor?"

Camille shrugged again. "My client states the child raided his mother's alcohol pantry while my client was out checking on a noise he heard. There was no intent to harm the child, nor was there any direct provision of alcohol to the minor. It was a simple oversight, nothing more."

Tony kept his face neutral, but he wanted to scream. The only witness that could testify against Damien was the child himself, but he was too young to be considered a credible witness in a court of law and Camille knew it. "I think you missed your calling, Ms. Sanders."

She raised an eyebrow and tilted her head slightly. "Oh? And why is that?"

He forced a laugh and closed the case file. "You should have been a writer with that incredible pile of fiction you just pulled out of thin air for Mr. McKnight. There's just one question I have. If the two ladies in question supposedly hired Damien to do all this stuff to them in order to act out their fantasies, what would their motive possibly be for turning on him and crying that it was forced?"

Camille leaned back in her chair and that short, smug smirk reappeared on her face. "That, Detective, would be your job to figure out. Perhaps they were ashamed to admit the truth to their brother. Perhaps they were gold diggers looking to get a portion of Damien's sizeable inheritance. Whatever their motive, my client should be released immediately. There is no case here. Presenting yours to the judge will be a waste of everyone's time."

She was most likely right about that, but Tony would present his case to the District Attorney anyway. He switched his gaze to Damien, whose face echoed the smug expression of the lawyer.

He gave Damien a short, tight smile as he collected the files in front of him. He hesitated for a moment at the door. "It's too bad the courts are so clogged with cases. Takes hours, sometimes days, for the proper paperwork to make it through. And that, of course, assumes that no accidents happen or that the paperwork doesn't get lost. I'm sure you know your way out, Ms. Sanders. Damien, the deputy will be here in just a moment to escort you back to your cell until the proper paperwork is filed."

Camille stood up and followed him out the door. "You can't hold my client if you aren't going to charge him with a crime. You know that!"

Tony's abrupt stop meant Camille was forced to take a step back or collide with him. He turned around to face her. All that was between them was Damien's case file.

He kept his face neutral and his voice as calm as possible despite the fact he wanted to reach over and throttle the woman. "I can't just release your client, Ms. Sanders, until the proper paperwork has been filed. You know that. There are procedures and processes in place, all of which I am certain you studied during law school. Now, if you will kindly see yourself out so that I can get back to the work you want me to do, I'll be on my way."

~ ~

"McKnight. You're being released." Damien stood up hastily and ignored the rest of his cellmates as he walked forward.

He'd spent 72 hours in that hell and he was going to make Zhara and Gabby pay for every minute of it. He kept his mouth shut, though, as he claimed his things from the evidence desk.

His motorcycle was in the impound. They'd given him a claim ticket but he would have to pay the $300 a day fine to get it out. That infuriated him. One more thing Zhara and Gabby owed him.

The lawyer was good, he had to admit. He'd felt pretty hopeless about his case until he called on her. "I call it the 50 Shades Defense. It's been working like a charm for my clients who find themselves in similar situations. There's no definitive proof for them to offer that says the two ladies didn't ask for it, so if you come back and tell them it was a verbal arrangement to fulfill their desires and you're the victim, the courts have nothing they can do about it. The system requires that the people prove your guilt. You don't have to prove your innocence."

That was probably the best $2500 he'd spent in his whole life. Worth every penny just to not have to see the inside of a jail cell for longer than they'd already made him.

Camille's warning to him was one he was going to ignore, though. "Once you get out of that jail cell, stay away from the ladies. Do not go near either Zhara or Gabby. The police are going to be watching you like a hawk. They are going to be working very hard to prove that you're lying about this. You come around them, you do anything to them, and you'll be falling right into their hands. I won't be able to save you the next time the way I did this time."

The way Damien saw it, Zhara and Gabby owed him. They owed him for the money he'd been forced to spend to defend himself and to get his bike out. They owed him for the humiliation of being handcuffed and tossed in a jail cell like some common criminal. He'd been through hell these last few weeks. It was high time he returned the favor.

The question was when and how. What was the best way to hurt them, to make them feel every ounce of his pain and then some, without having it blow back on him?

He took the turn off into town and passed by a faded sign that pointed down the road with the words "This way to Purgatory" scrawled on it. A slow grin spread across his face. That was his answer.

He'd always hated how close they were as a family. It made him feel even more lonely and unwanted just watching it. He'd hated their grandfather, too, with his holier-than-thou attitude whenever he'd come to visit Zhara back when the old man was still alive.

He'd forced himself to hold back a smile the afternoon Zhara'd come home to find the bastard dead. He thought he'd finally have Zhara all to himself, but that was before Mike and Gabby showed back up and tried to turn Zhara against him.

She'd finally given into them and abandoned him, found herself a new man, but he wasn't about to let her go like that. Mike and Gabby had taken everything from him. It was their fault she didn't love him anymore. If he could get rid of Mike and Gabby, he could make Zhara come to her senses.

Zhara ran to Purgatory every time they got in a fight. She ran to Mike and Gabby every time she got hurt. If he took Purgatory away from her, she wouldn't have any choice but to run back to him. If Mike and Gabby didn't have Purgatory, they wouldn't stay in that town. They'd move on and it would be back to being just him and Zhara, just the way he liked it.

Purgatory was going to burn. The only question was when.

Chapter 32

"Run, run, run, as fast as you can, Zhara girl, you're never going to get away from me." Damien grinned as he took the largest rock he could find, wound up for the pitch, and threw it as hard as he could toward the bar's front window. The throw was perfect and he was rewarded with the satisfying sound of shattering glass.

He walked up to the window and kicked the rest of the glass in before using it as his impromptu front entrance. No need to open the front door and risk setting off an alarm that might spoil his fun before he could finish what he intended to do.

He stood still for a moment, waiting for his eyes to adjust, before heading toward the bar. He knew exactly what he needed. The room was still and silent. He could hear every step of his boots on the wooden floors. A grin stretched across his face. There would be plenty of noise soon enough.

He stepped behind the bar and grabbed a half-empty bottle of whisky in one hand and a bottle of scotch in the other and proceeded to alternate between drinking from the bottle and splashing it liberally all over the floors and counters.

He emptied those, threw them against the wall, and grabbed two more. He wanted to make sure that there was absolutely nothing left of this place.

The wooden floors were thirsty and soaked in everything he poured on them almost as fast as he could pour it. "Four down. 121 more to go."

An hour later, he grabbed a rag from behind the bar and surveyed the damage. The place reeked of alcohol and the fumes were making his eyes water. This place was going to burn hotter than hell.

He pulled his lighter out of his pocket and strode toward the door. He was a half foot from the front when he lit the left-hand corner of the rag. He intended to toss it behind him, but the rag burned faster than expected. He yelped as the heat of it scorched his fingers and he dropped it.

The whoosh of flames catching on to the alcohol that was soaking his boots and the cuffs of his jeans were his first indication that he was in serious trouble. In less than a minute, he was engulfed in flames. He screamed in panic and reached for the door.

He'd forgotten it was locked. He turned toward the open window to climb out but a sudden breeze blowing in fanned the flames, until a wall of fire surrounded him in every direction.

~ ~

"I can't wait to get things settled so we can move back there."

Mike smiled at Gabby. It was nice to see her in such a good mood.

"Yeah, it'll be nice to get a fresh start. I'm going to miss Purgatory, though."

Gabby sighed and shrugged. "There are things I'll miss about it, too, but….oh, my God. Mike, is that fire?"

The orange glow on the horizon was accompanied by an unmistakable plume of smoke that hovered above the town. Wildfires were a fairly common occurrence in the high desert but were usually far enough outside of town not to cause serious concern. This looked like it was coming directly from the area of the town.

"Check the weather report. See if there's been a report of a recent outbreak of wildfires."

Silence descended as Gabby checked her phone. "No. Nothing reported. Let me call 911."

She dialed the number as the mile markers ticked away. "9-1-1, please state the nature of the emergency."

Mike listened in as his sister made the report.

"We are aware of the emergency, ma'm and firefighters have already been dispatched to the area. Thank you for your report."

Mike tried to keep his eyes on the road. "At least they know about it. With all that black smoke, though, I would venture a guess they haven't been able to contain it yet. Let's just hope it doesn't spread."

Gabby nodded. "Do you think Zhara will be okay hanging out in Reno for a while?"

Mike looked over at his sister and smiled. "I think Zhara can handle herself. She'll be fine. Besides, John seems to be a good influence on her. It was nice of his sister to invite her to stay with her for a few weeks."

Gabby sighed. "Maybe if Zhara's out of town, Damien will find someone new to obsess over once he realizes she's not coming back to him."

Mike hoped so, too. That relationship had caused enough damage. "Hopefully now that he's being watched by the police, he'll think twice about coming around."

They reached the turn-off to Purgatory, but there were fire trucks and barricades blocking the way.

"Gabby, stay in the truck. Let me go find out what's going on here." He parked the truck and headed toward the barricade. He recognized a familiar face.

It was Manny, one of his former teammates, standing watch. "Manny, what's going on here? Can I get through?"

Mike's stomach dropped when Manny didn't quite meet his eyes. "Mike, it's Purgatory. The whole place went up in flames. And, there's more. They found a body inside. It's too badly burned for them to be sure it was him, but Damien's bike was found in the parking lot."

Mike felt the blood drain from his face. He shook his head in disbelief. "Tell me you're joking. Please tell me you're joking."

Everything they had of value was in Purgatory. He felt like he'd been sucker punched in the gut.

"I wish I were, man. I wish I were."

How was he going to break this news to Gabby? How was he going to tell her that everything was gone? Every memory, everything they owned except the truck he was driving, the clothes in their suitcases, and the cash in their wallet was gone. All of it.

He walked back to the truck slowly, trying to gather his thoughts. There had to be some words he could say to make things better. There had to be something he could do to make this nightmare more bearable. All he could think, though, was that Purgatory was gone.

~ ~

Gabby watched Mike's interaction with Manny and knew within minutes that something was very wrong with this situation. Mike's entire demeanor changed. His shoulders slumped and his face looked older and more weathered as he drug himself back to the truck. She felt her stomach clench as she waited for him to open the door and share the news with her.

"It's all gone, Gabby. It's all gone."

She looked at him and shook her head, not understanding. "What's gone, Mike?"

His eyes fixed on hers. "Purgatory and everything in it. It's all gone."

Her whole body began shaking, as if all the warmth from her body had suddenly departed. "Everything?"

He dropped his head to the steering wheel and wouldn't look at her. "Everything."

Words escaped her. She didn't know what to say. It was so unreal to her she couldn't quite wrap her brain around this. "How?"

That was all she could manage. Knowing the answer wouldn't change anything. It wouldn't magically restore Purgatory or give them back their things, but it was the first step in making sense of it all.

"They aren't sure yet, but Damien's bike was found in the parking lot and there was a badly burned body in the bar."

Gabby's eyes widened and she stared at Mike. "Thank God Zhara's not here."

She watched as Mike turned his head briefly. Their eyes locked. "Thank God none of us were here."

The realization that they could have lost so much more than Purgatory if not for the trip to Reno hit her. They could have all been dead.

"Where are we going to sleep?" Gabby couldn't help but voice her concern. She was tired, Purgatory was destroyed, and it was much too late to get a hotel room for the night. Most of the check in desks were closed.

"I don't know. I don't know."

The two sat in silence, watching as the smoke finally turned from a dark black to a dull grey and eventually to a pure white.

Manny strolled over as the firetrucks began to pull out from the scene. "Mike, Gabby, the fire marshal says it's not going to be safe for you guys to start looking through for another couple of days. There are still embers and cinders that could ignite, and the police want it kept clean until they have a chance to look for more information about the body."

Gabby felt a bubble of panic rise up in her. "Where are we supposed to stay, Manny? Where are we supposed to go?"

He looked uncomfortable. "I wish I could help, Gabby, but I'm afraid there's nothing I can do."

She felt tears forming at the corners of her eyes. Mike's voice cut through. "Thanks anyway, Manny. We'll handle this."

He waited until Manny walked away before he turned to Gabby. "We should inform Zhara, at least about Purgatory. Maybe she can let us borrow her place for a few nights."

Gabby nodded. Hope rose. Zhara would never say no to them. Especially not on a night like tonight.

"Of course. You can stay at my place for as long as you need to. It's going to be a little cramped, but we'll make it work. I can't believe Purgatory's gone. I mean, I know we were going to sell it, but to have it just gone? It's. I can't believe it."

Nobody can, Gabby thought. Nobody can.

Chapter 33

"Damien? He's dead? You're sure?" Zhara sank back on the chair that she was sitting. Nothing in her body or her brain felt like it was working right.

"All they told us was they found a body and Damien's bike was in the parking lot. The body was burned too badly for it to be identified immediately. I'll let you know when we know more."

Gabby's voice came through the other line, but Zhara couldn't process it. Anger, grief, sorrow, and regret all warred with a sense of relief and hope. The relief and hope sparked a wave of guilt that washed over her. What kind of person could love a man for six years and then suddenly feel relief and even hope after finding out that person was dead?

She'd never wanted Damien to die. She'd just wanted him to stop hurting her. "It's my fault. If I just hadn't found John, Damien would never have done this."

Gabby's voice was angry and sharp when she replied. "Don't you dare. Don't you dare take responsibility for this. This is NOT your fault. You are NOT to blame. You didn't light those matches. You didn't break into our home and set our whole place on fire. Damien did."

Gabby's reassurance of her innocence did nothing to beat back the growing sense of responsibility for the tragic situation. "He wouldn't have done it if I hadn't…"

Gabby cut through her sentence. "Stop. Just stop right there. You spent six years making excuses for everything Damien did to you, to us, and to our family. No more. You are not responsible for what he did. He is."

Gabby's accusation of her making excuses triggered a wave of anger. "You never liked him or approved of him. You hated him. You wanted him to go away and now he's dead."

Gabby was quiet this time, her voice cold like ice. "Don't blame this on me, little sister. I warned you about him. You wouldn't listen. I don't blame you for what happened, but I am not going to take the blame for this. You're damned right I wanted him to go away. The man nearly raped me and put my family through hell. I'm not dancing on his grave, but you won't find me shedding tears over his death, either."

The sudden reminder of what Damien had done to Gabby came like a slap in the face, jolting her out of her anger and pummeling her with a renewed sense of guilt. Gabby would never have gotten hurt and Damien wouldn't be dead now if not for her.

"I hurt everyone I touch."

The thought crossed her mind even as her ability to speak was choked off by the tears that threatened to burst from her like water from a dam. She could scarcely breathe. Gabby's voice broke through the silence.

The hurt and the disbelief Gabby felt were evident in the way she spoke. "You're not speaking to me now? Is that it? Over Damien?"

She wanted to speak but she couldn't. Gabby's voice was laced with anger and sorrow. "I don't need this right now. Call me when you remember who your real family is."

Gabby hung up. Silence filled the room, leaving Zhara with only her thoughts. She felt more alone than she'd ever been in her life. Gabby and Mike would never understand the grief she felt over Damien's loss. She doubted that John would understand it, either. She hardly knew John's sister, Kathy, let alone well enough to seek comfort in the woman's arms or to share her burdens with her.

There was nowhere to go with everything she felt. She'd intended to stay here in Reno for a few weeks and spend some time with John, but that no longer seemed the right thing to do. She needed space and time to sort through everything. She hoped John would understand, but even if he didn't, she couldn't be with him right now.

She stood up and started packing her bags, fighting back the tears that fought to break through. She hated crying. It was a sign of weakness, and she hated feeling weak.

~ ~

"Please tell John I'll call him when I'm able."

Kathy looked up from the kitchen table where she was sipping her coffee to find Zhara standing there with bags in hand. Her eyebrows rose and she was confused. "Did I do something wrong?"

Zhara shook her head but her eyes never rose from the floor. "I – there's been a problem at home and I need to go."

Kathy set her coffee down, compassion replacing confusion. She stood up and moved closer to the girl. "Oh, sweetheart. I'm so sorry. Is there anything I can do to help?"

Zhara's brown eyes finally connected with her own. She looked miserable. "Just…tell John I'm sorry."

The earlier confusion returned, and Kathy sensed there was something more that was going on here. "Sorry? For what? A family emergency? I know John will understand…"

Zhara shook her head and again, turned around, and walked out the door without another word. Kathy followed after her. "Zhara, whatever it is, just talk to him. I'm sure he will understand."

She watched as a driver pulled up and Zhara opened up the back door. "Please. Just tell him I'm sorry, okay? I'm sorry for everything."

Kathy shook her head and headed back inside to grab her phone. "John, I think you should call Zhara. She just left. She said something about a family emergency, but I think there's more to it than that."

~ ~

John called the number for Mike, hoping the man would pick up. He had a lot of respect for Zhara's older brother, and he was fairly certain he would know exactly what was wrong with Zhara. "John, hey, I guess news travels fast, huh?"

John frowned in confusion. "News?"

Mike sighed. "I take it you didn't call about the fire, then?"

John frowned. "Fire? No, Zhara just mentioned some kind of family emergency."

Mike's voice sounded tired. "While we were in Reno, Purgatory burned to the ground."

John's eyes widened in shock. "Thank God you guys are okay!"

There was a pause on the other end of the line. Mike's voice sounded strained. "Okay is not the word I'd use. Alive, but not okay. We lost everything."

John's heart hurt for them. "I can only imagine how you must be feeling right now. Will the insurance be able to cover the losses?"

There was another brief pause on the line.

"Oh, my God. John. Thank you. I need to go. Thank you."

John stared at the phone in bewilderment. He wasn't sure what he'd done to warrant thanks. "Wait, I was —"

But all he heard was silence on the other end of the line. "I was hoping you could tell me what was wrong with Zhara."

He spoke to the empty air and shook his head. With Purgatory burnt to the ground, he was almost certain that Zhara was headed back to meet up with Mike and Gabby. He would likely find her somewhere along I-80 if he hurried.

~ ~

"Gabby, I think we're going to be okay after all."

Gabby looked up from her seat by the window. She'd been reading a book, but her attention was suddenly focused on Mike. "How so?"

Mike sat down beside her. "Insurance."

She blinked for a moment and the light of hope reached across her face. "I didn't know we did. Isn't that policy old?"

Mike nodded. "It is. Grandpa's the one who set it up, but it was set to autopay. When he died, I just let it keep going."

Gabby frowned. "Are we sure it will transfer? I mean, if the policy was his, can we file a claim against it?"

Mike pursed his lips for a moment, thinking. "It should. The policy was on the place, and since we have proof of Grandpa's death – or, more to the point, can get that proof – we should be able to prove that we are the rightful heirs of the insurance."

Gabby leaned back in her seat and put her book down. "Do you know which insurance company he went through? I mean, that was all a blur to me back then. I was just struggling to come to grips with the idea that Grandpa was dead."

Mike stood up and started pacing. "It should appear on the bank statements for Purgatory. Like I said, it was set to automatically deduct from the account and I never changed it. If I look at the bank statements, we should be able to figure out who he had his policy through and what we need to do to file a claim."

Gabby took a deep breath. For the first time since the fire, there was hope on the horizon, but she didn't want to let herself buy into it too soon. There were still a lot of variables to work through. The policy might not transfer the way they thought it would. "Wait. Do we know who Grandpa named as beneficiaries of the policy?"

Mike paused for a moment, then shrugged and continued pacing. "No clue. To be honest, I never even looked at the policy. I don't know what's in it, what it covers, or who is set to get paid if it's filed against. All I know is that it exists and that it's been paid consistently since Grandpa died, so it should be possible to file a claim."

Gabby allowed that thought to sink in for a moment before looking up at Mike. "We may get to Reno a lot sooner than Spring."

Mike gave her a brief smile. "We just may. God help him, but Damien may have just done us all a couple of favors in spite of himself."

Chapter 34

"Thank you." Zhara waited for the driver to finish retrieving her bag from the trunk before walking toward the train station. Her steps were slow and her heart was heavy, but this was the best way back home. Once she got there, she'd reclaim her motorcycle and head to Grandpa's for a while. At least, that was the plan. Of course, lately her plans hadn't been going so well.

She walked up to the ticket counter to buy the train ticket to Winnemucca. That was the closest stop to Purgatory.

"Our earliest train leaves out at 4:06 pm. Please arrive at least 1 hour ahead of departure."

Zhara thanked the woman at the counter and paid her money. It was going to be a long wait. Reno only had one train in and one train out. The bus no longer ran between Reno and Winnemucca, flights didn't exist between the two, and it was far too expensive to try getting a lift from someone to take her that direction even if she could find someone willing.

Calling John was out of the question. She didn't want to hurt him, and she wasn't sure he would understand why Damien's death hit her so hard. To everyone else, Damien was like a tornado. He came into their lives unexpectedly and without welcome, destroyed things, and then left nothing but a giant mess to clean up. But Damien was more than that in her eyes.

He was the first person who seemed to really understand her. He wasn't with her because he felt sorry for her. As much as she loved Mike, Michaelle, and their Grandpa, that was the reason for their relationship with her. They felt sorry for her. They didn't need her. She needed them.

Damien understood what it was been like to feel like you didn't have a home and you didn't belong anywhere. He'd made sure to give her a key to his house and to tell her she was welcome anytime. Many was the time she'd taken refuge in his house when things with Grandpa got too tense, and he'd never once turned her away or asked questions about why she was there.

For the first two years of their relationship, he'd never even tried to have sex with her. If she came over, he would sleep on the couch and let her have the bed. He'd made her feel beautiful and wanted without making her feel like she owed him anything. He treated her like an adult and let her make her own decisions about things.

She'd known, even then, that he was seeing other women. He never slept with those women at his house, though, or gave them a key. That made her feel special.

He'd stuck up for her when his friends would come over to hang out, too. He made sure they included her and made it clear to them that she was under his protection when she was under his roof. He'd taught her how to defend herself with a knife after she told him about a guy at school that had tried to force himself on her. She wasn't sure Damien was responsible for it, but that same guy came to school the following day with a broken arm and a few bruises on his face, and also made sure not to come near her anymore.

There were a thousand things that Damien had done over the years to endear himself to her. A thousand things that nobody but she ever saw or heard from him. Those things were the things she grieved. It was that side of Damien that she would miss the most.

It was like there were two Damiens living in the same body. She'd fallen in love with the good Damien, but once things were starting to get really good between the two of them, the bad Damien would show up and ruin everything. That Damien couldn't stand for anybody to be happy, let alone Damien himself, and seemed to take a perverse pleasure in hurting anyone who dared to get near him.

She'd spent six years trying to rescue the good Damien from the bad Damien, but the constant struggle had worn her down and she'd gotten tired of fighting. John was everything she'd loved about the good Damien without all the drama from the bad Damien. However, that just confused her.

She'd known why the good Damien had needed her. He'd told her as much one time after one of their breakups.

"I don't know why I keep driving you away. I need you. When I'm with you, I want to be a better man. I don't know if I can change, but I know that I want to change."

Those were the words she'd clung to during difficult moments in their relationship. But in the last year, she'd stopped believing the words were true. She'd stopped believing that she had any kind of power to reach him. She'd gotten to the point where she was running on empty.

John filled her cup. Every time she was with him, she walked away feeling better about herself, her life, and her future. There was something about him that gave her hope and made her begin to believe in a better tomorrow. She didn't know what that something was, but she knew it was something she wanted. She just couldn't trust it.

She didn't know why John needed her. She didn't know what made John want to be with her at all. What would keep John from deciding one day to just up and leave? How could she be sure that he wouldn't get tired of her and go find someone else? If a person didn't need you, why would they want you at all?

John's love for her was a complete and total mystery. She wasn't sure she would ever understand it. It certainly wasn't something she'd earned or nor was there something she'd done to cause it. He seemed to simply just give it without expecting anything in return. That's what made it so hard for her to trust it and believe in it. She didn't trust anything she couldn't understand.

~ ~

John grabbed the car keys and headed out the door. Zhara's bike was still back at her home. She'd traveled to Reno with Mike and Gabby. That meant there was only one way for her to get back home: the train station.

John pulled up to the station and parked. It would be hours before the next train pulled out of the station, and Zhara was travelling with her suitcase. It would be unlikely she'd wander far. There was still time.

He wasn't sure what was going on inside that woman's mind. She was a complete mystery to him. The minute he thought he was beginning to understand her, that is the minute she changed. It was both infuriating and exhilarating at the same time.

He climbed up the steps and opened the doors. He took a few minutes to spot the curly dark head seated on the far end with her back turned toward him. Part of him was relieved to have found her.

At least he knew she was safe. Part of him was deeply hurt. Why not call him and ask him to take her home if she needed to leave? Didn't she trust that he would understand?

He crossed the distance between them and sat down beside her. "Is this seat taken?"

She looked up and her eyebrows rose slightly. She gave a small, tight smile. "Didn't your sister tell you I was leaving?"

He leaned forward and kept his eyes on her. "Yes. She did. I came because I wanted to know why you didn't call me and tell me directly. I thought we'd agreed we were going to give our relationship a chance."

She looked away then and then at the floor, carefully avoiding his gaze. He waited for her to speak, both afraid to hear what she would say and needing to hear it at the same time. "Damien's dead, John. At least, they're pretty sure it was him. The body-"

Her voice choked up slightly and he waited for her to recompose herself. "The body was burned too badly for them to be sure."

Suddenly, her behavior made sense. "You're grieving for him."

He didn't say it to accuse her, merely to recognize her pain. He hoped she would see it that way.

She looked at him, then, and nodded. "I know it may seem crazy after everything he's done, but I loved him, and I can't help feeling like it's my fault he's dead."

John reached for her hand. She allowed him to take it. "Zhara, did you think I would be upset with you?"

A slight frown touched her lips. She shrugged. "Gabby is. Maybe Mike, too."

John could understand that, too, in a way. Gabby was still struggling to work through what Damien had done to her. She wasn't in a place to see anything good about the man.

John held her gaze. "Your capacity to love, Zhara, is part of what draws me to you. That you are able to see the good in Damien and love him in spite of his unlovable behavior is part of what I admire most about you. There aren't many people who can do that."

Her eyes closed and twin tears leaked from her eyes to trace a path down her face. "He wasn't always like that, you know? He could be so gentle sometimes, so sweet."

John listened as she poured out the story of their relationship. He didn't interrupt her or try to stop her. He just absorbed her words and the pain that came with them, allowing her to get it all out of her.

When she was finally finished, he sat there with her in silence for a few moments. "Zhara, what do you need from me? Please be honest with me. What do you need?"

She wiped the tears from her face and blew her nose into the handkerchief he'd handed her midway through her story. She didn't speak for a few moments. "I don't know, John. I think, maybe, I just need a little time to figure everything out."

He felt his heart sink, but he tried not to let it show. He didn't want her to feel guilty for asking for what she needed. "You planning to go back to your place?"

She shook her head. "Mike and Gabby are staying at my place, and

Gabby, well, she doesn't get it. She told me to call her again when I remember who my real family is. The thing is, John, I know they're my family, but I can't help how I feel about Damien."

He squeezed her hand. "Of course. So where will you go?"

She sighed then and looked back down. "There's this place my grandpa – my real grandpa – left me. It's just a small cabin out in the middle of nowhere, but I think it's exactly what I need right now, you know? Time, space, and a place to think."

John nodded. It did sound like a good place for her. Maybe what she needed most right now was to reconnect with her roots and figure out who it was she wanted to be moving forward. "It sounds lovely. How long do you think you'll be there?"

Zhara shrugged. "Honestly, I don't know."

He gave her a small smile. "Well, if you'll collect your things, I'd like to take you there."

She looked at him then, the surprise written all over her face. "I could never ask you to –"

He cut her off. "You didn't ask me. I offered. Please, Zhara. Let me take you home. I know you need time alone, but I'll feel better if I at least know where you are.'"

She nodded and glanced up at him. "You're sure?"

He smiled then and reached for her bag. "I'm sure."

Chapter 35

John slid into the driver's seat and closed the door just in time to hear Zhara say, "You don't have to take me home if you don't want to."

He started up the car and shook his head. "Zhara, I wouldn't have offered if I didn't want to."

She bit her bottom lip and then turned her face away from him to look out the window. "But it's so far out of your way."

He glanced briefly at her. It was clear she had no idea what she meant to him. "It will bring me a great deal of peace of mind to know you are safe and to know where you are."

She shook her head and her voice trembled slightly. "I don't understand you."

That was only fair. He didn't understand her either. However, he wanted to understand her thinking so he asked her anyway. "What do you mean?"

She took a moment before speaking, as if to gather her thoughts.

"I don't understand why you seem to care so much. I mean, all I ever seem to do is cause you trouble."

His heart broke for her. "Is that how you see yourself?"

She didn't hesitate with her reply. "Well, yes."

John kept his eyes on the road but what he really wanted to do was pull over and hold her. "You don't see yourself at all, do you? You have no idea the kind of power you hold."

Her eyes grew round and her mouth opened slightly as if she were about to speak but then she shut it again and swallowed before finally saying, "Power? What are you talking about?"

He chuckled slightly. "The power to launch a thousand ships if that's what it took to bring you back home. You're so full of light and life that you draw me to you like a moth to the flame."

She snorted and crossed her arms over her chest. "Great. So you're telling me I'm doomed to draw men to me only to burn them up and kill them. If that's power, you can keep it."

He recognized the somewhat unfortunate metaphor he'd chosen in light of Damien's recent demise. "I'm sorry. I didn't mean to hurt you. That's not what I'm trying to say at all. I'm telling you that you have the power to set men's hearts on fire – whether for good or for evil. It's entirely up to you how you choose to use that power."

Her voice cracked slightly when she responded and he could practically hear the pain oozing from it. "So Damien was my fault?"

He sighed, frustrated with himself for being unable to adequately communicate to her what he wanted her to see. "My God, no. Damien made his own choices in how to respond to you. What happened to him as a result was tragic for everyone involved, but it certainly wasn't your fault."

Zhara's voice was bitter and sharp. "Then why do I feel like it's my fault? Why do I feel like I am to blame for all of this?"

John took his time thinking through his response. He knew that he both needed to comfort and reassure her, but at the same time to help her see the truth of both who she was and who she could become. "Because you've been in a habit of accepting responsibility for Damien's choices in life the entire time the two of you were together. You took responsibility for his happiness and you blamed yourself for his unhappiness, too. But the truth is that while you did exert a tremendous influence over him, you were never capable of making Damien happy nor were you ever responsible for it."

Her silence was the only reply she gave him. He began to wonder if he'd somehow hurt her with the things he'd said. He glanced over at her to find tears streaming down her face. Her eyes briefly connected with his and she closed them tightly. He allowed her the space to gaather herself.

"I tried. I tried so hard. I couldn't do it. I couldn't make him happy, John. I can't make anybody happy."

John reached a hand over and rested it on her knee. "It was never your job to make anyone happy except yourself, Zhara. It's not your fault they weren't happy. It wasn't you that was the cause of their unhappiness. They weren't happy because they were looking outside of themselves for the happiness they desired. Happiness is a choice we make, a choice to find the positive in the middle of the negative and to bring good out of every bad thing. It's not an easy choice, nor is it easy to hang onto, but it is no one's responsibility but our own to make us happy."

Her response to his words flew like an arrow straight into his heart. "But when they aren't happy, they leave, John. They leave and then I'm all alone."

She broke down sobbing then, drawing her knees to her chest and burying her face in them. He wanted to hold her, but he knew that she wasn't ready for that. She would push him away if he tried. "Oh, Zhara, is that what you believe? That you have been alone?"

She nodded, the curls bouncing every direction, tears soaking the legs of her jeans.

"One day, I hope you realize that you have never been alone. Love has been with you all along. You might not see it, but it surrounds you."

She said nothing, but her sobs gradually subsided into shuddering gasps that eventually gave way to calmer breathing. "If it was there, I couldn't see it or feel it."

He smiled briefly. "Did you not? Did you not taste rain drops or feel warm sunshine on your skin? Did you not see sunrises and sun-sets? Hear birds chirping and smell the clean, fresh air? Those are all the signs of love that let you know you are not alone. You are never alone, Zhara, unless you choose to shut your eyes to the beauty of the world around you and block it out."

She looked out the window again and slid her legs back down, stretching them. "How do you do it? How do you stay so relentlessly positive?"

John chuckled. "I have my dark moments, too, Zhara. Moments where the darkness feels so deep that I doubt I'll ever climb out and I catch myself longing for life to end. It's just that I've learned to recognize those moments as precursors to a greatness I haven't yet seen. I remind myself that winter may be dark and it may be cold, but it only lasts a season. The night might be long and it might be deep, but it eventually gives way to the day."

He stopped for a moment and reflected before continuing. "Then, I pour out my pain into the keyboard and I use it to write something beautiful that I can share with the world. I turn my darkness into a gift I can share, something that will bring hope and smiles and beauty to others. That's how I do it."

Zhara glanced over at him. "How is it you can make hurting so badly you wish you were dead sound like such a beautiful thing?"

He shrugged. "It is beautiful in its own way. That I can hurt so badly means I can love that deeply."

She looked away again and sighed. "You are an amazing man, John Huntsman. I could spend a whole lifetime just trying to understand you and I don't think I would get any closer than I am now."

She was right, of course. That was the beauty of any relationship. No matter how hard you tried to learn everything there was to know about a person, there was always so much more to know than you could ever discover.

He grinned and shifted gears as he slid into the turn. "Is that a proposal?"

She snorted. "Hardly. More like a lifetime sentence."

Well, at least she was in the mood to joke. That was an improvement, he supposed. "I would gladly be sentenced to a lifetime of loving you, if you were willing to have me."

She glanced over at him and shook her head. "You don't deserve that kind of punishment."

His heart gave a short, brief lurch but he'd been asking for it. He knew it was too soon for her. She needed time to heal, not pressure to enter into a commitment.

He thought of his father's words to him back when he'd been a lovesick 13-year-old with dreams of wedding a girl he'd met at school. "If you love a girl, Johnny, there are three things you need: patience, persistence, and prayer. Pray for her daily so she's never fighting her battles alone. Be patient as you wait for the right timing for the two of you to be together. And be persistent. Never let her forget that she is wanted, desired, and loved."

It was good advice then, and it was good advice now when he was eleven years older and madly in love with a woman whom he was 99.9% certain was the one for him. She just didn't know it yet.

Zhara was a one-of-a-kind original, as different from him in background and personality as two people could possibly be, and yet there was an undefinable quality about her that made every other woman he knew pale in comparison. He'd met many women in his travels as a musician, some more lovely and more beautiful than Zhara, but none with the power to capture him so completely and captivate him.

He would be patient for as long as it took for her to see that his love was real and not going anywhere. He would continue to pray for her for the rest of his life whether or not she ever agreed to be his wife. And he would make sure that she knew, in every way that it was possible for him to let her know, that she was loved, wanted, and desired.

Chapter 36

"I just can't believe her, Mike. I can't. How can she do this to us? To me?" Gabby scrubbed at the tears trickling from her eyes, wiping them on her jeans.

"Gabby, I don't think –"

She glared at him and he stopped, taking a deep breath instead. "Don't. Just don't. Don't make excuses for her, okay?"

He could hear the hurt and pain in her voice and knew that he was just making himself a target for all of that if he kept going, but he couldn't help himself. "Gabby, come on. It's not like that. You know it's not."

Her face was turning splotchy red, a sure sign of danger ahead. He steeled himself for her temper. "You always take up for her. Why can't you take up for me this time? Why can't you be on my side?"

He held up his hands in defense. "Gabby, I am on your side. I've always been on your side. You're not the only one hurting in this, you know?"

Those words just seemed to set her off even more. "You don't know what it's like for me. You don't understand what I've been through! And for her to do this?"

He forced himself to relax. Getting upset with her wouldn't help anything. "She's not doing this to you —"

Gabby held up a hand and turned away from him. "I don't want to hear it, Mike! She IS doing this to me! She's doing it to you. She's doing it to all of us. I just wish you could see it the way I do."

He put a hand on her shoulder. "Stop, Gabby. She's not Mom, okay? She's not Mom."

Gabby shrugged it off and turned back around to him. Her eyes were glittering dangerously, and her voice was sharp and shrill. "This has nothing to do with Mom! You can leave her out of this, Mike!"

Mike crossed his arms and refused to back down this time. "Oh, I think it has everything to do with Mom. You think Zhara is choosing Damien over us just like Mom chose the bottle over us, don't you?"

Gabby clenched her teeth and practically screamed the next words at him. "She is! She is choosing that piece of garbage over us! You didn't hear her. She was telling me that maybe if she hadn't left him that fucking loser would still be alive. Then she tried to tell me if I'd have just accepted and approved of him, he wouldn't have been the way he was. Do you get that? It was somehow my fault because I didn't approve of and accept his abusive behavior!"

Mike shrugged. "She's not thinking straight, that's all. She's just a kid, Gabby."

Gabby poked a finger into his chest. "She's not a kid anymore! She hasn't been a kid for four years, but you still treat her like she is. Maybe if you stopped treating her like a kid and started holding her accountable, she wouldn't be in this mess now."

Mike stepped back and shook his head. "Oh, so it's my fault now?"

Gabby crossed her arms and glared at him. "She looks up to you, Mike. She'd have listened to you."

Mike snorted. "You seriously overestimate my power over Zhara. She listens to me about like you do – when it suits her and no other time. I warned her about Damien, but she didn't listen to me anymore than she listened to anybody else."

Gabby seemed to lose all of her energy at that. She slid down to the couch and put her head in her hands. "I wish I'd never met Damien. God, I just wish I'd never met him."

Mike took a seat beside her and put a hand on her back. "Yeah, well, there's nothing you or I can do about that."

She leaned against him. "He ruined EVERYTHING! He ruined things for me in high school and he just kept on ruining my life every chance he got. Why couldn't he leave me alone? I never did anything to him!"

He put an arm around her shoulders and gathered her close. "I know, Gabby. But guys like Damien can't take that. He wanted your attention. He wanted you to notice him."

She snorted and shook her head. "He wanted me to sleep with him, and when I wouldn't, he made sure every decent guy in school thought I had. I guess he thought if I had no other options, I'd coming running to him and give him what he wanted."

Mike nodded. "I doubt he ever really forgave you for that. It's not Zhara's fault, you know. She didn't know all that stuff. She didn't know who he really was."

He saw Gabby's jaw clench as she spat the words out. "I tried to warn her, Mike. I did."

Mike gave her a tight hug. "I know, Gabby. I know."

They sat in silence for a few moments until Gabby spoke again. Her voice was barely above a whisper. "I couldn't save her. I tried. I couldn't."

He knew without her having to say so that she wasn't talking about Zhara anymore. "I know you did, Gabby. It's okay. You couldn't save her because she didn't want to be saved."

He felt her tears moisten his shirt, and her voice trembled slightly. "Grandpa said that, too, you know. He said that after she lost Dad, she just didn't want to be saved anymore. He kept trying to help her. But she didn't want help. I think she just wanted to be with Dad."

He felt his own tears welling up as he thought back to those days. Those were dark days he tried not to dwell on too often. "Maybe. I don't know. All I do know is we couldn't stop her. Just like we couldn't stop Zhara and Zhara couldn't stop Damien."

They sat there a moment longer in shared misery before Gabby voiced a question he'd never thought to ask himself before. "Why do we love people who can't love us back?"

He shook his head. He wasn't sure there was an answer to that question. "I don't know. I wish I did."

~ ~

"My bike is over at my apartment. You can follow me to Grandpa's place, or you can head back home to Reno. It's up to you." Zhara glanced over at John, trying to figure out what he would do.

He gave her a brief smile. "I'll follow you. I want to make sure you get there safely."

Zhara reached for his hand. "I'd invite you to stay with me, but I think I need a little time and space to think things through."

It was hard for her to say the words, hard for her to risk him getting impatient with her and finally deciding to give up on her, but she knew she had to say them anyway.

"This might surprise you, but I agree with you."

A tiny arrow struck her heart. Was he that eager to be rid of her? She tucked a strand of hair behind her ear and tried to hide the hurt she felt. "Oh? Why's that?"

John kept his eyes forward. "Zhara, right now your heart still belongs to Damien. You loved him, and it is going to be a challenge for you to lay that love to rest so you can make room for a new love. I want you to come to me when you're ready to let go of him and make room for me, and not until then."

Zhara pursed her lips and frowned. "But what if I take years? Will you still be waiting for me?"

John reached out a hand and patted her knee. "I would wait for eternity if that's what was required. Take your time. I'm not going anywhere."

Zhara's frown depeend. "But you're missing out on other women, on a family, on everything. Why would you wait for me? What if I never come around?"

John glanced her direction before returning his eyes to the road. "My father once told me that I would know it was true love when I could leave it behind, certain I would never see it again, and yet every road led me right back to it again. And more than that, when you get back there to where you left love behind, it's still waiting for you. That's how he knew for sure my mom was the one. Every road always led him right back to her, and when he returned, she was still there waiting."

Zhara sighed. The words sounded sweet, but they were also starting to make her feel uncomfortable and afraid of disappointing him. The last thing she wanted to do was hurt him. "That sounds romantic, but it also sounds hard and painful."

John squeezed her hand briefly. "For the right person, the pain of waiting is worth it. And, of course, I'll have my music to keep me company. You just focus on healing, and I'll focus on playing, and when the time is right, we will find our way back together again."

Zhara found herself frustrated by his words, as if he weren't really listening to her. She felt bad that she might be setting him up for disappointment. "I don't want you to wait, John. Try and find somebody who can love you back. I don't know if I can. I don't know if I ever will. It's pointless for you to wait for me."

John was silent for a time, and she thought perhaps he wasn't going to answer her. "I am sorry. I don't mean to put pressure on you to make a commitment you aren't ready to make. Please forgive me."

She shook her head, dark curls tumbling every direction. "You aren't the one who owes an apology. All you've done is try to love me. It's me, John. I'm the broken one. I'm just sorry you picked me to love."

He sighed then, a small sigh, and smiled at her but the smile didn't touch his eyes. "I have no regrets. And if you ever need me, at any time, for any reason, no matter where you are or when you call, just know that I will be there."

Zhara shook her head and stared out the window. "What did I do to deserve someone like you?"

John's reply startled her. "You don't deserve love. Nobody does. That's what makes it so magical. You know you don't really deserve it and then along it comes anyway. It lifts you up, renews you, restores you, and changes you. Once you've been touched by love, your life is never again the same. Love is a gift. You don't earn it, you don't deserve it, you just receive it."

Zhara shook her head again and returned to looking out the window. "I doubt I will ever really understand you, John Huntsman."

Chapter 37

"Zhara?" Mike turned toward the door as it opened and watched as a sheepish Zhara slipped in followed by John. The man seemed decidedly uncomfortable to be there. He couldn't blame him.

"Hey, Mike." Zhara's answer was soft enough he barely heard it. He guessed she was worried about waking Gabby.

"You coming home?" He looked at John, although the question was directed toward Zhara, trying to assess the situation between the two of them.

She shook her head. "No. Just here to pick up a few things. I think it's best if I give Gabby some time…"

Mike frowned. "She doesn't need time, Z. She needs to know you love her. She needs to know you've still got her back the way she had yours when you needed it."

Zhara's amber eyes darkened as they snapped to his face and her voice rose. "How could she even doubt that, Mike? Everything I did for the last few weeks was to protect her. I can't help that I loved him. I hate that he did those things, and especially that he did those things to her, but I can't help what I felt for him and I won't apologize for feeling. I won't."

Mike sighed. "I'm not asking you to, Z. I'm just asking you to think about it from her point of view."

Zhara stiffened as she headed toward her bedroom. "I am thinking about it from her point of view. That's why I'm leaving. I can't help how I feel, and I know she can't help how she feels about him, either. I'm no good at faking my feelings and I'm not going to."

Mike looked over at John. "She staying with you?"

John's eyebrows rose and he shook his head. "No. I'm just here for moral support. She was worried about an encounter with Gabby."

Mike's frown deepened. "Even dead that man keeps causing my family trouble. I just wish those two could work things out."

John took a seat. "They will. They love one another. They just need time to heal. Perhaps Zhara going is for the best, at least for now. It'll give her a chance to sort out her feelings about Damien in a space where she does not feel judged for what she feels."

Mike crossed his arms over his chest. "Is that what you think is happening here?"

John held Mike's gaze. "I think it's how Zhara sees things. She feels as if she's being judged to be a bad person because she loved the wrong person and is now grieving the loss of that love."

Mike stared at John for a few moments before looking away. "She's not a bad kid. Damien had her fooled, that's all. He didn't deserve her love and he doesn't deserve her grief."

John glanced in the direction of the closed bedroom door and lowered his voice. "Nobody does, Mike. Love is never deserved. It's always a gift and a surprise. That's what makes it so marvelous. We don't deserve it and we know it, but we receive it anyway."

Mike grunted but said nothing else, waiting for Zhara to re-emerge. It took a few minutes before she came back out with a backpack, her grandpa's rifle, and a duffle bag. Mike reached out and pulled Zhara into a hug. She was stiff at first, but then relaxed. "No matter what happens, Z, you'll always be one of us." He could feel damp growing on his shirt and he kissed her on top of her head before letting her go.

She didn't look back as she walked out the door, but John stopped and shook his hand. "I'll let you know when I drop her off."

Mike nodded. "Do you know where she's headed?"

John shook his head. "She mentioned it's her grandfather's place, but she didn't tell me more than that."

Mike's eyebrow rose. "Her grandpa's place, huh? Makes sense. At least I know how to get ahold of her to let her know where we're going when the time comes."

~ ~

Despite the tension of the moment, Zhara broke into a grin when she saw her motorcycle parked outside the apartment building. "You are a sight for sore eyes." She couldn't wait to mount up and ride out. It'd been too long since she'd felt the wind in her hair.

She dropped her bags beside the back tire and began strapping her grandpa's rifle to its side. "Time for me to take you home."

She was so intent on what she was doing that she jumped when she felt a hand on her shoulder. She relaxed as she looked up and spotted John's face.

"You ready?"

She stood up, grabbed her bags, and slung them across the back. "I am."

The drive through the cool morning air was more than enough to help her catch her second wind as she drove up the highway. Her pace was slower than usual. She was careful to make sure that she kept John in her rearview mirror. She didn't want to lose him.

She pulled off the highway and onto the dirt road leading up to the cabin. Things were exactly as she'd left them. The porch swing began a light swinging as she dismounted the bike, as if her grandfather were welcoming her back home. It made her feel safer somehow thinking that he was watching over her in his own way.

John parked and got out. "So this is the homestead, eh?"

She nodded. "It's not much, but it's mine. I haven't lived here since I was a kid, but I've missed it."

She took a seat on the swing and patted the space beside her. "Why don't you come swing with me?"

He chuckled and took a seat. "You sure you're going to be safe out here?"

She shrugged. "No place is ever safe, John. But I'll be safe enough. I've got my grandpa's gun if I need it and I know a few other tricks, too."

He frowned at the word gun.

She raised an eyebrow. "You don't like guns?"

He hesitated. "I understand why people own them, but I don't like them."

She raised an eyebrow. "What do you do for safety and security? Aren't you worried about break ins and things like that?"

He shook his head and reached into his pocket, pulling out a strand of crystal beads with a crucifix dangling from the end, and brandished it in front of her. "This is my weapon of choice. It never misses."

She rolled her eyes. "More like it never hits. You try fending off a mountain lion with one of those things? Let alone a human predator?"

He smiled, "Don't underestimate the power of a rosary in the hands of one who knows how to use it. Your weapon has – what – a maximum of 6 shots before you need to reload? Mine doesn't run out of ammunition."

She glanced at him. "My mouth doesn't run out of words, either, but I wouldn't trust that as my only line of defense."

He nodded. "It's not my mouth I'm trusting, or my words. You see, every prayer I say with the rosary puts an arrow in the hands of my guardian angel. And my angel's aim is unfailing. It never misses its target."

She looked out at the overgrown fields where her grandfather had died so many years ago. A thorn of bitterness lodged in her heart. "Yeah? Well my angel must have been asleep on the job."

She stood up and leaned against the front porch railing. "Where was your mother's guardian angel when she needed one? Or mine? Or my grandfather's? Or my mother's? Where was God in the middle of all of this? If there is a God, He has a lot to answer for."

John stood and joined her. "Right where He's always been. With us, walking with us, doing His part to work all those things that people intend for evil to our good."

She crossed her arms over her chest. "I don't see how any of this has worked out for our good."

She could feel his gaze on her. "If none of this had happened, you and I would never have met and I would not be standing here now. You wouldn't be part of my life and that, to me, would be a true tragedy. Besides, Zhara, this is a story that's still being written. Every would-be hero must go through plenty of trials in order to grow into the person they must become to defeat the villain."

She gave a short, sharp laugh at that. "I'm no hero, John. Just one mixed up mess of a woman who brings trouble to every person whose life she touches. And I don't see that changing anytime soon."

John sighed. "We're all mixed up messes in our own way. The only difference is that some of us own it and others of us refuse to admit to it. That you own it is a good sign to me. It means you're honest with yourself about where you are, and that's a place to begin building."

She shook her head. "Begin building what?"

He stepped off the porch and onto the stone path. "A future."

He turned around to face her and held out the rosary. "I know you don't believe, but I'd feel a lot better if I know you have one. I'll get you a booklet from the car that explains how to use it. It's saved my life more times than I can count. It might save yours, too."

She hesitated. She didn't really want to take it. She didn't see the point, but she thought she'd hurt him enough. There was no point in being even more unkind. She reached out a hand and he coiled the rosary in her palm.

She watched as he walked to the car and opened the glove box, pulled out a small booklet, and brought it to her. "Everything you need to know about how to pray it is in here."

"Mike and Gabby's grandpa was big on praying the rosary. It's been a few years, though. I've forgotten how the prayers go. I stopped praying it when I started dating Damien."

He smiled and his next words, she was absolutely certain, weren't entirely about the rosary. "It's okay. It'll come back to you. No matter how long you've been away from it, it'll always be ready for you when you come back to it."

Silence stretched between them and Zhara wasn't entirely sure what else to say or do. She wanted to invite him to stay but knew it would be a mistake. She needed time to herself where she could sort through her thoughts and feelings without the complication of a relationship. Fortunately, John seemed to recognize that it was time to go.

"Call me if you need anything. Anytime, anywhere. No matter the time of day, no matter the distance. Just call, and I'll be there."

She wasn't sure how to respond to that so she gave him the only answer she could. "Thank you, John. For everything."

It was hard watching him drive off down the road. There was part of her that wanted to stop him and tell him to come back, but she didn't. He was better off without her, and it would be sheer selfishness to convince him to stay just so she would have somebody to cling to. It was time she learned how to stand on her own. It was time to grow up and take care of herself.

Purgatory was gone. Hell was dead. Heaven was waiting for her, but she had a long way to go before she felt worthy of that.

Reviews Appreciated

If you enjoyed this book, please consider leaving a review wherever you purchased it. Reviews, along with purchases, are used by sites to determine what books to promote and which to bury. Furthermore, reviews help other readers decide whether or not to give an unfamiliar title a try.

Writers use reviews to help decide whether a project is worth continuing, if the work is a series, and to decide how to make the next work better. It is one of the best ways to thank an author if you enjoyed the time they took to create it.

Other ways to thank an author are to, of course, spread the word by mouth or reach out directly to the author and let them know your thoughts.

If leaving a review seems intimidating, or you aren't sure what to say, here are some questions to use:

1) What did you like most about the book?

2) What did you like least about it?

3) Were there any places where the narrative felt unbelievable?

4) Was there any place where the narrative lagged or lost your attention?

5) What was included in the book that you wished hadn't been?

6) What wasn't included in the book that you wish had been?

7) What was the most meaningful or memorable moment in the book for you?

8) Were there any places where you found yourself confused or uncertain about what was happening?

Fan Fic Welcome

This may be due to publisher copyright constraints, but many authors not only discourage fan fiction, they actively hate it. I am not one of those authors.

I encourage fan fiction. I will happily provide you with a free guide to the characters and the world in which they live if you email me at 40daywriter@gmail.com using a subject line: [End of Purgatory] Free Character Guide.

When you've completed your fan fiction writing, I ask that you submit it to me for review at the same address using a subject line of [End of Purgatory] Fan Fiction + "Your Title". This will alert me to the book the fan fiction is attached to and that it is fan fiction.

If I read it and approve it, I will offer you the option to work with me and will help you publish and promote it. If I read it and do not approve it, I will let you know why and what changes you would need to make in order to get it approved.

Those who are interested in writing fan fic and sign up for the guide will be invited to join a weekly fan fic club where we can discuss works in progress, get feedbacks and critiques, and dive into potential story ideas and lines.

About the Author

International speaker and award-winning author, Brandy M. Miller, wrote her first book in 2004, and published her first book in 2012 and currently has ten published titles in addition to this one.

Prior to this book, her focus has been on writing non-fiction with a few children's fiction titles.

The devastating impact of narcissism on relationships and families is something Brandy is intimately familiar with as she is herself a recovering narcissist.

Connect with Brandy Online:

Join her live stream on Twitch (http://twitch.tv/mistressofportals) every Tuesday from 3-6 pm CST, Thursday from 7-10, and Saturday from 1-4 pm. She can usually be found telling stories through game play and just having a good time.

She can also be found on Twitter @WriterBrandy, Instagram @ DesignerBrandy, Facebook (BrandyMMiller1975), and LinkedIn

Other Publications By This Author:

How to Write an eBook in 40 Days (or Less)

Creating a Character Backstory

The Write Time: How to find all the time you need to write a book

The Poverty Diaries: Excerpts from the diaries of someone who's been there

The Secret of the Lantern: A choose-your-path adventure for Catholic kids

7 Steps to Change Your Life & the World

I Wish I Could Draw Like That: Life lessons learned on the journey to becoming an artist

Turning Problems Into Profits

Lucy the Candle

Lucas the Candle

I Am the Candle

Leading Trends Magazine (http://leadingtrends.biz)

Printed in the USA
CPSIA information can be obtained
at www.ICGtesting.com
JSHW021913030324
58127JS00009B/35

9 781948 672214